D0386369

Alpine Meadows Nurse

Also by Colleen L. Reece
in Large Print:

Everlasting Melody

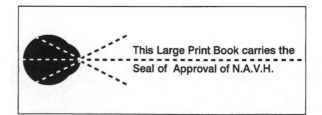

This Large Print Book carries the
Seal of Approval of N.A.V.H.

ALPINE
MEADOWS
NURSE

Colleen L. Reece

HM6148
18.95
AF-LT
6/97

Thorndike Press • Thorndike, Maine

Published in 1997 by arrangement with Colleen L. Reece.

Thorndike Large Print ® Candlelight Series.

The tree indicium is a trademark of Thorndike Press.

The text of this Large Print edition is unabridged.
Other aspects of the book may vary from the original edition.

Set in 16 pt. Plantin.

Printed in the United States on permanent paper.

Library of Congress Cataloging in Publication Data

Reece, Colleen L.
  Alpine meadows nurse / Colleen L. Reece.
      p.   cm.
  ISBN 0-7862-1081-8 (lg. print : hc)
  1. Large type books.   I. Title.
[PS3568.E3646A65   1997]
813'.54—dc21
                                                              97-9866

For my faithful four —
Darcy and Missy Hedal,
Kelly and Tara Lawler

Chapter 1

The shining engagement ring spun on the small table and was still. It reflected in its depths the tears in the eyes of the white-uniformed woman who had slowly removed it from her hand.

"Kelly! You can't mean this!"

Her dark eyes looked into those of the doctor across the table. "I never meant anything more in my life." There was a finality in her voice not to be questioned, almost a deadness.

"But why? You know you love me, have always loved me. Why, Kelly, why?"

She was silent for a long moment. "I think you know why."

He flushed, dropped his head, then looked at her. "Because of what happened? What other choice did I have?"

"I suppose for you there was no other choice."

He seized her words, desperately clutching them. "Then you'll put your ring back on and we'll be married as planned." He reached for her hand, but she moved it away, folding it in her lap.

"Kelly!" He stared at her. "Can you say you don't love me anymore? Can you look me in the eyes and tell me that? It's the only way I'll ever let you go."

The tears had vanished from her dark eyes. Now they held only pain and sadness. "No, I can't say I don't love you. Perhaps I always will." With a quick motion she was on her feet. "I do know I can never marry a man I don't respect — and I no longer respect you."

With a swish of white skirt she was gone, leaving the young doctor alone at the table, helplessly watching her vanish down the long hall.

"Nurse Lawrence, what's this I hear about your resigning from the hospital staff?" It wasn't a question, it was a roar. The chief never spoke in tones less than thunder when he was upset, and he hadn't been this upset in weeks.

Kelly Lawrence, R.N., nodded her sleek dark head, perkily carrying the nurse's cap that looked so much like an upside-down cupcake.

"I suppose it's because of that unfortunate business." Even the chief could not withstand the look Kelly gave him.

"I prefer not to discuss the past — any of it," she said.

"Look here, Kelly, there's no need for you to leave! The whole thing will blow over in a few weeks. You'll be married and —"

He was cut short. Kelly held out a bare hand, only a narrow band of white against the suntanned fingers showing where a ring had been worn.

"You've broken your engagement?"

"Would you have expected me to do anything different?"

The chief sighed. "I suppose not. But are you sure about this?"

"Quite sure." She abruptly abandoned the subject and leaned forward. "Now I'm wondering if you know where I can get a new job. I know you have contacts all over. Do you know of anyone who needs a children's nurse?"

"Where do you want to go?"

"As far away from San Antonio, Texas, as I can get!"

The chief was shocked by her passionate outburst. Evidently she was taking all this harder than he had suspected.

"Give me a few days." He glowered at her under bushy brows. "Fine thing. Resigning from my hospital and expecting me to get you set up elsewhere!" The look of sheer misery in her face melted him. "Kelly, honey, he never was good enough for you."

"It doesn't help to think that, Dad." For the first time she acknowledged the relationship between them, then flew to her father's arms. "Nothing helps. That's why I have to get away."

The gruff chief of staff patted her hair. "We'll find you a job, one a long way from San Antonio. This has all come up so suddenly, everyone's off-keel." He sighed. "Maybe if your mother had lived, things would have been different. I didn't do such a good job as your dad and mom both."

"You did a fine job!" She stood up straight, her dark eyes shooting sparks. "I wouldn't trade you for anyone in the whole world, Dad. I'm just glad I found out in time. What if I'd already been married?" She couldn't hide her shudder. "How could a woman stay married to a man she didn't respect?"

"A lot of them apparently do." His answer was dry. "Personally, I hope you find a real man next time you fall in love."

"I will never, ever fall in love again, never."

"That's tempting fate, Kelly. Don't let your disillusionment with one cocky doctor turn you against love. I hope someday you can have the kind of marriage your mother and I had for ten years. Joy, hardships, moments of tenderness. All tied together by our love."

"You've never talked like this to me before, Dad."

"Maybe you've never needed it so much before, Kelly. I can't let you become bitter because life handed you a mean crack." He cleared his throat. "Now get out of here and let me do some telephoning. I'll be home for dinner."

Kelly managed a smile. "Then I'll fix a great steak and trimmings."

There was warmth in the look between them as Kelly slid through the door.

For a long time Dr. Lawrence sat staring into space, working his fingers. Not even to Kelly would he admit a touch of arthritis had been troubling him. He spent part of his free time flexing his fingers, keeping them limber for the delicate bone surgery he performed from time to time.

Where could he send Kelly? He reviewed all the hospitals that came to mind, shaking his head. What she needed was a chance to get into a completely different atmosphere, a place where she could forget, not be reminded by every turn of the corridor of her broken engagement. She needed to get away from a big hospital. Should she become a doctor's office nurse? No. It wouldn't satisfy her.

Far back in Dr. Lawrence's mind something was struggling to come alive. What was it teasing his memory? By extreme concentration, he helped it come to the fore. It was a letter, one that had just come a few days ago. He had skimmed it, not really taking time to read the whole thing. For a few moments he fruitlessly pawed the stack of correspondence on his desk, then gave up.

"Joan!" he roared. He wouldn't have ever really needed the intercom.

His secretary winced, covered her ears, and dashed through the door.

"Where's that letter? The one from Kirk Long?"

Expertly she unearthed it, smiled at his crestfallen "thanks," and returned to her typewriter. He didn't even notice when she left. He was too engrossed in the letter.

"Well, Dad, did you think of where I could go?"

Kelly and Dr. Lawrence relaxed in front of the fireplace after dinner. She had kept her word. The steak and all the trimmings had been great. She loved to cook but didn't have the opportunity often.

"Actually, I think I have found a place."

"Really?" She leaned forward eagerly, her languor disappearing. "Where am I going?"

Dr. Lawrence looked at her intently. "You look like your mother used to when she was excited." He glanced at the picture above the carved mantel, the laughing dark eyes and hair, the white dress from another day.

With an effort he returned to the present. "Kelly, how would you like to spend a summer out of doors?"

"Outdoors? You mean a vacation?" She lit up. "The two of us?"

He hated seeing her enthusiasm die as he said, "Sorry, honey. I can't get away. No, this would be an outdoors job."

"But what can a nurse do outdoors?"

It was Dr. Lawrence's turn to lean forward. "I can offer you a job that will include swimming in a mountain lake, hiking, horseback riding, and campfires. It includes cookouts, tall trees, sunlight, time to lie on pine needles and look at a blue sky."

"You mean at a guest ranch or something?" Kelly was doubtful. "But I'm a children's nurse."

"Not a guest ranch." Dr. Lawrence was enjoying himself. "Kelly, a long time ago, when I was first getting into bone-specialist work, I helped a child who had had polio. I

13

know it seems incredible now when just about everyone gets vaccinated. But somehow this boy hadn't been vaccinated. The reason why doesn't matter. I don't think I ever knew.

"It was a bad case and when it was all over, he was crippled. But, Kelly, that kid was the toughest little guy I ever knew! When some of the staff thought he'd never walk again, he up and told us he'd not only walk, he'd run and hike and do everything else any other boy could do. The fantastic thing about it is, he did just that. He fought a thousand defeats. And when I last saw him, he only had a slight limp. By now, it's probably almost disappeared."

"But what does it have to do with me?"

"I'm coming to that. After all these years, I got a letter from him." Dr. Lawrence pulled a battered-looking envelope from his pocket. "It's a wonder it ever reached me!" He pointed to the many forwarding addresses, then slipped the letter from the envelope and began to read.

Dear Dr. Lawrence,

You may be surprised to hear from me after all these years. You may not even remember me, but I remember you. You were the guy who believed I could walk when everyone else gave up. I'll never forget the extra hours you spent with me, helping me exercise. I didn't know then it wasn't part of your job. I guess I wanted to walk so bad I just took it for granted everyone was there for my exclusive benefit.

After I got through school I went into forestry and have spent the past several years working outdoors. You'll remember how crazy, how almost fanatic I was about the outdoors. The outdoors and Alpine Meadows.

Dr. Lawrence broke off reading. "Alpine Meadows. I hadn't thought of that name in years. Kirk used to tell me about it during our sessions together. Seems his grandparents had settled in the Mt. Rainier area in Washington State. They acquired quite a piece of land not far from a little place that later became Alpine. I understand it's now a charming small town.

"Anyway, the Longs built a huge log house, cleared part of the land, and left much of it in trees. There's a small lake, a view of Mt. Rainier that is just short of spectacular, and miles of trails."

Kelly could feel her interest growing. Could this be connected with the job Dad

15

had mentioned? He picked up the letter again.

My grandparents are dead. Gramps died just a few months ago. When the will was read, I found Alpine Meadows had been left to me. Some of the other cousins are furious, but Gramps said in his will, "Kirk loves Alpine Meadows. I trust he won't sell it."

All of this is just a buildup, Dr. Lawrence. To get to the point, there isn't enough money in the estate to keep taxes paid and so on without my working. If I keep on with the Forest Service, I'm subject to transfer. I've been doing a lot of deep thinking. The result is a resignation from the Forest Service.

I'm going to turn Alpine Meadows into a sort of halfway house for kids who have had bone diseases, or any kind of affliction or operation on their legs or spines. I believe in this atmosphere they'll make a real attempt to do things they wouldn't do at a hospital. The lake will provide swimming. There are trails both easy and hard. I'll even keep a few horses for those who progress to the nearly well stage.

Dr. Lawrence, it was the thought of

getting outside, of being normal again, that pulled me through. If I can spend the rest of my life helping other kids the way you helped me, it will be the realization of a dream. I'll only charge what they can pay. If someone can't pay, they won't be barred.

The only thing I lack is medical help. I know you wouldn't leave your practice. But do you know of a young doctor, or even a highly qualified nurse, who would like to spend a summer at Alpine Meadows?

It will be small this year, not over twenty patients. I've already lined up a cook/handyman husband-and-wife team. I'm having two one-story dormitories built this year.

I've secured two counselors, one for boys, one for girls. And I'll be getting a second set of counselors. Alpine isn't far away and there are qualified doctors, even a hospital, there.

What I really need is someone who will take on a more or less round-the-clock job. We'll be taking kids from about six to sixteen. Homesickness may be a problem, so I need someone who can assist the counselors, as well as take care of whatever else comes up.

I wish you would plan to come visit us sometime. I'll certainly appreciate any suggestions.

Sincerely,
Kirk Long

Dr. Lawrence dropped the final page of the letter. He wasn't prepared for the on-slaught of his daughter.

Face shining, she threw herself to the rug in front of him. "And you think I might get to go?"

"No, I don't think you might get to go."

The color and hope died from her face.

Dr. Lawrence chuckled. "There's no think about it. I called Kirk Long this afternoon. He was overjoyed. He will expect you as soon as you finish out your notice here, get packed, and fly to Seattle. You'll be picked up there."

"Oh, Dad!" She sighed in relief. "What a wonderful place to go! It's perfect." She stared at the fire, picturing the flames chang-ing to a campfire, with singing and fun.

Then a thought stopped her. "Dad, did you tell this Mr. Long you were sending your daughter?"

"No, I didn't, Kelly. I wanted to discuss it with you first. I told him I knew of an excellent children's nurse and would approach her. I'm to confirm your arrival time when arrangements have been made. Why? Do you want to go incognito?"

"I don't know." Her eyes were troubled. "He idolizes you so much I'd hate to just be accepted on your merit. I'd like to stand on what I do. Would that be dishonest? At the end of the summer I could tell him who I really was."

"I think it's a good idea, if you feel that way," Dr. Lawrence said, surprising her. "Use your middle name, Lee. It's got the same initial as Lawrence, so your luggage will be properly marked. Of course, all this isn't necessary. But if you want to — well, why not? By the way, Kirk has the same initials. Don't get confused because of it."

"I won't." She looked up at him. "What do you think he's like now, this Mr. Long?"

"I would guess just what his name implies, long. He was tall for his age, freckled. He had sandy hair and blue eyes. I would imagine he's rather craggy and outdoorsy. A real man."

Something in her father's voice brought Kelly bolt upright. "Dad, is there something you aren't telling me?"

"Like what?" His face was bland, his eyes innocent.

"I don't know. Like maybe you have an idea for another romance for me." Her face whitened, her eyes stood out. "I don't want Kirk Long falling in love with me."

"Good heavens, Kelly, the man may be married! Besides, even if he's single, what makes you think he'll be trailing around after you? He sounds to me like a man who has his life planned. He must be in his late twenties or early thirties now. If he isn't married, he might never intend to marry!"

"Sorry, Dad!" The first real laugh Kelly had given all day bubbled up, washing away some of her hurt. The future lay ahead. Why borrow trouble? "As you say, he probably isn't just sitting out there waiting for me to arrive and bowl him over."

She didn't catch the smile on her father's face as he busied himself poking the fire into a brighter blaze. She was too busy planning aloud. "I'll have to check my clothes and —" She broke off.

"What is it, Kelly?"

"Most of the clothes I have are my new ones, my trousseau."

"And?"

"And I'm going to enjoy wearing them! Except, how do you wear dress-up clothes working at a children's camp? We had planned to go on a luxury cruise." Her lips trembled.

"Forget the trousseau. I'll give you a check tomorrow so you can get what you need. I'd suggest several pairs of jeans, shirts for both cool and hot weather, hiking shoes, a good raincoat, a heavy jacket, and lots of socks. You might throw in one or two of your dressier outfits. Seattle isn't that far away. You might be going down there sometimes."

"You know, Dad, in spite of all the challenge ahead, I can't just forget the past."

"No, you can't." He looked tired, defeated for a moment. "But the thing that will help you most is that you're doing what you know you had to do. When a person's right, it's a clean break. I believe a clean break is the only way to start healing. Even in our profession it's true. It's the splintery ones, with jagged pieces sticking out, that don't heal."

"Thanks, Dad." Kelly's eyes were wet. "Sorry for the sudden tears." She lifted her chin. "Forward with flags and the beat of drums." With a gay little salute she marched to her room.

It was long after midnight when the telephone rang. Dr. Lawrence automatically reached for it on the bedside table. Before he said hello he heard his daughter's voice.

"You? Why are you calling me this time of night?" she asked the caller.

"I just got off shift. I heard on the grapevine you might be leaving the hospital. You can't do it, Kelly, you can't!"

Dr. Lawrence couldn't have released the phone if all his hopes of heaven rested on it. His fingers tightened, leaving sweaty prints. But the crisp voice of a girl who had inherited her mother's beauty and his decisiveness reassured him.

"Yes, I can, and I am. What's over is over. Good night."

Dr. Lawrence gently cradled the phone, smiled, and turned back to his pillow. If Kelly could speak like that, she would be all right.

By the time Kelly finished out her notice at the hospital and packed, it was late May. Greenery traced the white adobe home she had known so long, and the sun was already hot.

"It isn't easy, leaving home and you." The upward curve of her lips was subdued that day at the airport.

"It never is." Dr. Lawrence had reverted to his usual gruff self. "It will be good for you to get out on your own."

"Heavy father, huh? Pushing baby bird out of the nest?"

"Why not? Baby bird should be able to fly by now." But his sternness was belied by the forlorn look in his eyes. "Kelly, if all goes well, how would you like me to fly out this fall when Alpine Meadows closes for the winter?"

The brilliance of her dark eyes dazzled him. "How grand!"

"Don't tell Kirk," he warned. "Something might prevent it."

A voice from a loudspeaker was calling, sounding mechanical and bored. "Last call for flight to Portland and Seattle. Please board at Gate 7."

" 'Bye, Dad!" A quick hug and she was gone.

She had refused to let him go with her to the boarding gate. Before she rounded the corner, she turned and waved, her bright red suit making her look like a cardinal.

He waved back, then brushed an unaccustomed moistness from his eyes. It was as she had said — forward with flags and the beat of drums.

Chapter 2

The giant jetliner touched down, lifted, touched again, and slowed, coming to rest at the end of the runway. Kelly slowly gathered her purse, jacket, and small flight bag. It had been a good flight, clear, sunny.

She had caught glimpses of fascinating cities, the Grand Canyon. Usually they had flown too high for the glimpses to more than tantalize her. Someday when she had the money and time, she would go to all those interesting places.

In the meantime, wasn't she starting a brand new life in a brand new world? The beauty of Mt. Rainier in the distance as they had flown into Seattle had left her almost speechless. Nothing like that in Texas, much as she loved it.

Her cheeks were almost as scarlet as her suit as she entered the waiting room. She was to wait there for Kirk Long. The paging system was droning out its constant messages.

"Paging Kelly Lee. Paging Kelly Lee. Report to baggage area."

It took Kelly at least three pages before she

recognized it as being for her.

"I'd never make a good crook," she muttered to herself, lights dancing in the dark eyes. "I can't even remember that I'm Kelly Lee, not Lawrence, for this summer!"

The laugh at herself lingered in her eyes as she stepped to the baggage area.

The first person she spied was a man who fit Dad's projected image of what Kirk Long would be. Tall, craggy, a shock of sandy brown hair, a flash of blue eyes as he looked through the crowd, stopped on her for a moment, then traveled on.

"Just what the doctor ordered!" She laughed at her own whisper and approached the man. Dad had been right. He was long, long and tall. Yet her first thought as she looked into his eyes was, *I bet he would never save his own skin at the expense of a woman.*

"Mr. Long?"

"Yes?" He was as remote as an igloo and about as warm.

"I'm Kelly. Kelly Lawr-Lee."

"You?" His deliberate appraisal of her infuriated Kelly. "Well, I certainly was expecting someone much older and more experienced."

For one horrible moment Kelly was tempted to turn her back on him and catch the next plane to San Antonio. Yet she didn't come from fighting Irish stock for nothing. Raising her chin, desperately attempting to keep the red flags of color from staining her white face, she said, "I have been working with children ever since I finished training. I have the experience."

She didn't notice his initial shock give way to admiration for her courage in standing up to him. If there was anything Kirk admired, it was a person who stood tall. He hid his little smile. "And how long has that been, Miss Lee? Six months?"

Suddenly Kelly realized how ridiculous they sounded, standing at the baggage counter trading short sentences. She relaxed, laughed, and put out her hand. "I'm twenty-three, Mr. Long. I really do have experience with children as I'm sure Da-Dr Lawrence wrote and told you."

His white teeth gleamed. "Truce. Oh, by the way, Miss Lee, do you stutter?" This time there was no mistaking the twinkle in his eye.

"No-no." She joined in his laughter. "Well, only when I'm a bit nervous."

He expertly claimed her luggage before answering. Loaded with cases, he led her to the parking-lot exit, then stowed her gear in the station wagon marked *Alpine Meadows*.

"You'll have to forgive my boorishness,

Miss Lee." He slanted a glance at her. "On second thought, it will have to be Kelly. We aren't very formal at Alpine Meadows." She saw the scowl between his eyes. "It's just that I so badly want to accomplish what I've started out to do." His hands tightened on the wheel, expertly guiding the car into the afternoon stream of traffic.

Kelly could hear the longing in his voice. On impulse she put her hand over his on the wheel. "I understand, I really do. That's why I'm here. I've seen kids who need help come to the hospital. Some make complete recoveries. Others, with less wrong, never get back to normal. I want to be part of Alpine Meadows, too." In hot embarrassment she removed her hand and laughed a little nervously. "Sorry, I didn't mean to climb the soapbox."

Kirk cleared his throat of the huskiness her words had brought. "I'm glad you did. It's just when I saw you standing there, so stylish and everything —" He gestured helplessly.

Kelly's sense of proportion was rapidly returning. With an impish grin she drawled, "You ain't seen nothin', podner. These sure ain't my working clothes."

This time Kirk laughed outright. It cleared the air.

"Tell me about Alpine Meadows," she

asked. "Dr. Lawrence read me your letter and told me a little, but then he never saw it, did he?"

"Not yet. I'm still hoping to get him out here for a visit."

Kelly bit her lip to keep from blurting out he was coming at the end of the summer and contented herself with saying, "I know there's a lake and a log house and a lot of trees. But I know that can't be the real Alpine Meadows."

"It isn't." Kirk was silent for a long time. "Alpine Meadows is . . ." He shook his head. "It can't be described. I can't tell you of Alpine Meadows. I'll have to show you. Do you ride horses?"

"Me?" Kelly was surprised at the question. "I'm from Texas, remember? Of course, I ride."

"Okay, okay. But not all San Antonians ride, do they?"

"I suppose not. But I do. Dad and I rode a lot when we had time. He's going to miss me."

"Kelly, why were you willing to leave San Antonio and come clear out here to Washington State?"

She wasn't prepared to answer that. His words sent pangs of remembrance through her. "Well, I respect Dr. Lawrence a lot. He seemed to think it would be a good change for me, and —"

He cut her off. "It doesn't matter." If he noticed her confusion, he was too tactful to mention it. "The important thing is, you're here. And needed. As soon as we start getting the kids, you'll be swamped. I've never known a normal kid yet who didn't suffer enough cuts and bruises, even broken bones, to fill a hospital ward! You'll be more or less on call twenty-four hours a day. However, the dorm counselors will have full responsibility for the children, except for their health."

"What are your other staff members like?"

"First come the Cunninghams. They're an older couple. She's our cook. He does the outside work, helps with the horses and so on. They'll be Granny and Gramps to all the kids. Both are white-haired, energetic, and filled with love. They've been at Alpine Meadows since I was a kid.

"We'll have two sets of counselors or dorm parents, both married couples. Bob and Marilou Campbell are winners. They're a young couple, just been married a year or so. They want to do something more with their lives than just work and make a living. They're here already. Bob was a Boeing engineer, but they decided they wanted to work with kids. You'll like them. They're redheads in every sense of the word."

He was quiet so long, Kelly prodded him. "The other set of counselors?"

"I'm not so sure about them. Tom and Lydia Jackson were in my class at college. They married soon afterward. I'm not sure what it is, but I suspect Lydia wants more than he can provide. He's from Boeing, too. He'd been pushing himself, too much work, too much overtime. The doctor told him to take this summer off or he'd have a nervous breakdown. When he heard what I was doing with Alpine Meadows, he begged for the chance to be part of it. Lydia finally agreed to come along, but not with any degree of willingness. I thought I'd put her in with the older girls. Marilou will be perfect with the little ones.

"Kelly, I really didn't want the Jacksons here. But what could I do? I have a feeling this summer will be the deciding factor in their marriage. They'll be arriving soon. I hate to think they'll be just another couple who wind up on the scrap heap."

"Then you don't believe in divorce?"

"I didn't say that. I know there are cases where it's the only answer. But if I ever get married, she'll be stuck with me! Maybe that's why I'm still single." He took his eyes from the straight road for a moment. "How about you?"

"Oh, I don't ever want to have to go through divorce, either."

Kirk gave her a long, considering look, noting the telltale white band on her ring finger. "In the words of my grandmother, are you spoken for?" He flushed, wondering why it had suddenly become important for him to know.

"Not now." She didn't add anything else and a few minutes later covered a yawn. "My heavens, why do I feel so tired?"

"Don't forget, you're in a different time zone. It's two hours earlier out here." He glanced at his watch. "Five o'clock. Seven for you. How about some dinner?"

"I'd love it! I didn't realize how hungry I was!"

"Atmosphere or good food?"

There was an adorable dimple in her left cheek. It flashed now. "I'm all for the good food!"

"Now there's a gal after my own heart. We'll pick up a bite in Alpine and you can see our closest town. We're located just a few miles out of Alpine toward the mountain."

"I love the way you call Mt. Rainier the mountain, as if there were no other mountains anywhere around!" Kelly was gazing open-eyed out the window. "Everywhere I look I see mountains."

"Those? They're just hills."

"Not to a San Antonian."

"Wait until we climb some of them!" He swung into a less-traveled road.

"Dr. Lawrence said I'd get to hike. How can I be gone from Alpine Meadows?"

"Marilou is a dandy first-aider. She can keep an eye on things while you get time off. Besides, when you go, it will be with some of the kids. I don't want to call them patients."

"When do they start coming?"

"Not for another ten days, at least. The dormitories are almost finished, but I want a little time for the staff to get to know each other. It's vitally important that no personality clashes arise and upset our guests. I'm not worried about the Cunninghams or Campbells or even Tom Jackson. Lydia's another matter."

"We'll just have to keep her so busy she won't have time to get upset."

"I hope we can." For the first time a pessimistic note crept into Kirk Long's voice. "One thing. If she stirs up any trouble, out she goes, friendship with Tom or not." He broke off and braked. "Look!"

At first Kelly didn't see where he was pointing. Then she saw them. A doe, a buck, and two spotted fawns. They hesitated at the side of the road, evidently decided the car was no menace, and daintily crossed over, even stopping and looking at the two humans curiously.

"How beautiful!" Kelly's eyes filled with wonder. "It's been just too long since I've been outdoors where I love it."

"A week from now you won't be complaining of that." Kirk started the motor again. "We're almost to Alpine."

Kelly's eyes were wide. They crossed a flat space, then curved around a bit. Alpine was a small town, but not too small. A few busy streets provided necessary stores. There was a hospital and library and even a community education center.

"Green River College from Auburn provides an extension service here," Kirk explained.

By the time they were seated in a local restaurant, Kelly was starved. She was also learning a lot.

The waitress had greeted them with, "Hi, Kirk. New girlfriend?"

He didn't even blush, just smiled. "No. Nurse for Alpine Meadows."

The waitress smiled at Kelly. "Welcome.

We're all pretty proud of what Kirk's going to do."

Kelly had a strange feeling of coming home. "I'm glad to be here." She attacked her steak with her knife and fork. It was richly oozing brown juice, which delectably stained the baked potato. "Is this ever good!"

"You bet!" The busy waitress beamed at her again. "Nothing too good for our new nurse at Alpine Meadows. Say, Alpine Meadows Nurse. Sounds kind of romantic, doesn't it?" She slanted her glance at Kirk, but he just laughed.

When she had gone, Kelly whispered, "Is everyone so — so —"

"Outspoken?"

"I guess you could call it that."

"They're interested. They all know me. Have you ever lived in a small town?"

"No."

"You'll get used to it. When you live in a small town, you belong to everyone. They aren't nosy, just interested. A town like this depends on itself. If we get bad snows, we take care of them. We're about twenty miles from Auburn. We learn to take care of our own troubles. Don't mind what she said about being my girlfriend. She thinks I should get married like everyone else."

"Mind?" The good food and friendly atmosphere were restoring a self Kelly had thought dead. "I was flattered!"

Kirk threw back his head and laughed. "I can see we're in for a summer, all right!" He sobered. "Kelly, tomorrow morning after you get unpacked, I'd like to show you Alpine Meadows."

"Fine with me, boss. I'll be ready and waiting."

She was. The newly cut logs of her own little cabin at Alpine Meadows smelled so sweet she had drifted off to sleep almost before the light was out.

She loved the tiny cottage, with its minuscule bedroom, tiny bath, and larger room with two cots.

"For patients you need to keep overnight," Kirk had told her, then laughed at himself. "I mean, for guests you want here overnight."

"Kirk, why are you so insistent that they not be called patients?"

"For the same reason I'm asking you not to wear a white uniform or anything that looks like a hospital. I don't want these kids to see themselves as patients. They will all have been discharged. They need to see themselves as alive, healthy, strong. They need to see themselves as achievers."

He was silent for a long time. "That's the way I had to see myself, Kelly. It worked for me. I think it can work for others. I'm no Dr. Lawrence. I don't have medical training. I'll have to leave that to others. In the future, I hope to have a full-time doctor here, but for now I'll be taking kids who need the exercise, who can benefit from the outdoors. Some of them simply need to get away from parents who overprotect them, or won't encourage them to keep up an exercise program even when it hurts."

He brought his big fist down on top of the well-stocked medicine cabinet. "They have to keep on trying and trying! It's the only way some of them will be able to keep from becoming hopeless cripples, or from seeing themselves as such."

Now, in the early morning light, as Kelly dressed in jeans and boots, she thought of Kirk Long. Her hairbrush dropped with a clatter as she met her eyes in the mirror.

"Dad couldn't have known what he'd be like, but he was right. This is a real man," she murmured.

Her words seemed to hang in the air. She forced herself to look at the white patch of flesh on her ring finger. "As for you, once I'm outside more, you will fade."

A spasm of pain caught her again for what she had lost, but this time it was not so violent.

She thought of her final words the day she had given back the engagement ring that she had loved, the ring that had once promised a bright future. She had been right. She could never marry a man she couldn't respect.

What was it Dad had said? Something about even pain being easier if it came because you did what you knew was right?

"Breakfast!" A tap and call at her door roused Kelly from her trip to the past. Snatching up a bright bandana, she tied it over her hair and caught up a jacket. It was cold up here this time of morning.

"Well!" Kelly stared at the man lounging by her door. Gone were the "city clothes" he had worn to meet her at the airport. Now he had on a dark green shirt, pants, heavy boots scuffed from wear. "You look like something from the forest."

"I am. I'm the spirit of Alpine Meadows. You must be the sunshine." He glanced approvingly at the yellow shirt she'd chosen to go with her jeans, and at the matching yellow windbreaker.

"I love yellow. It's a happy color." She practically bounced along beside him. Even her own height didn't provide legs long enough to keep up with his big steps.

"Now you can see Alpine Meadows." He

stopped on a little rise of ground in front of her nurse's cabin and swept his hand over the scene in front of her.

Kelly was speechless. The panorama was beyond anything she had expected. Alpine Meadows more than lived up to its name.

Kirk watched her changing expressions, pleased. "Don't try to take it all in at once, Kelly. Let me help." They walked a short distance, then stopped. "That's the house my grandfather built."

It looked like a fort. Weathered logs rising tier on tier to form a gigantic house against the darkness of a hundred pine, fir, and spruce trees. Windows like eyes peering out on the world, sparkling with glass, softened by gently blowing white curtains.

"My grandmother planted the roses." Red, pink, yellow, white blooms with the growth of years, twining themselves around the porch posts, over the old-fashioned gate. Kelly's eyes could hardly take in all the color.

They left the log house, traveled on to two newer structures, also of logs, but half hidden by trees.

"Our dormitories. Each built to hold twenty, although we don't expect over half that many this year. I'll take you through them later. They're partitioned off, so in time we can separate age groups a bit better. They also have small rooms."

"How did you get those climbing roses there by the dormitories already?"

"Carefully! Mrs. Cunningham spent hours directing her husband and me as we transplanted them. We thought they'd give a feeling of home."

Kelly fought the stinging sensation behind her eyes. In an effort to rid herself of the wave of emotion threatening to break through, she looked past the dorms, past the stables and barn.

Through the trees she could glimpse a shining stream of some kind. She followed its path with her eyes, noting it emptied into a small but perfect lake. The dam inside her threatened even more and she threw back her head.

There it was. The mountain. She didn't even realize she had come to see it through Kirk's eyes. Snow-capped, magnificent, it seemed to rise from their very feet high into the air. She had never seen anything like it except in films. It was too much. Tears poured down her face.

"Kelly!" Strong hands turned her. "Don't you like it? Is it going to be too lonely out here?"

"Lonely!" She twisted from his grasp to face the mountain again. "I was just thinking.

How could anyone not get well here? When I think of the places I've had to take children back into, the crowded conditions, the lack of privacy or fresh air —" She couldn't finish. "Kirk, I feel as if I've come home!"

The man remained silent, watching her walk away from him in a need to be alone with her feelings. And deep in his brain beat a message: *Perhaps you have come home, Kelly, perhaps you have.*

Chapter 3

"My dear, how glad we are you've come!"

After such a greeting, Kelly walked straight into Mrs. Cunningham's arms and heart. She and her husband were everything Kirk had promised — and could she cook! Breakfast was hot biscuits dripping with butter, homemade raspberry preserves, an omelette lighter than air, and crisp bacon without a trace of grease.

"You don't eat like this all the time!" Kelly accused.

But Mrs. Cunningham just laughed. "Of course, we do. Wait until you spend a few hours outdoors. You'll be ready for lunch."

Kelly was to learn meals were a cozy affair, at least for now. When the guests came, a series of smaller tables would be installed in the big room of the old house that had been created from several smaller rooms.

For now the staff, including the Cunninghams, would eat around the old-fashioned dining-room table.

Bob and Marilou Campbell were also dears. Their twin red heads caused Kelly to wonder aloud, "How do you get along with so much red hair in one family?"

Marilou turned delighted eyes on her, then said, "We just say our say, then take it from there!"

Bob laughed. "You bet. I wouldn't trade Reddy here for anything."

There was so much genuine love and respect in his eyes, for a moment Kelly's fork trembled. Then she steadied her hand.

How long would it be that this pain in her heart would shoot up unexpectedly? What a contrast between the naturalness of the Campbells and the romance she had known. A romance of expensive dates, of glamorous nights, of elegant restaurants.

Marilou looked like a pixie in a denim outfit. Bob's well-worn jeans and shirt showed signs of contact with rough brush. Yet Kelly envied them, never knowing how her thoughts were reflected in her face.

Kirk could almost read her mind. Something had happened to Kelly. The white band on her finger shouted it had been fairly recent. He also saw how she had deliberately set her lips and regained control of herself. "We're riding this morning, Kelly, don't forget." He turned to Bob and Marilou. "You're welcome to come along, if you like."

"Not us." Marilou's red curls bounced merrily. "We have a few days before the kids start coming. I want Bob all to myself." She grinned at them all. "Not that I don't like you all. It's just that we haven't had much time since we got married just to be together. I think that's important." There wasn't a trace of apology in her voice.

"Good for you. Once the kids get here, and the Jacksons —"

Marilou interrupted him. "I still can't understand how come you asked them. Tom's a darling, but Lydia is something else! She tries to get every man from ten to a hundred."

"What would you do if she tried to get Bob?" Kelly wasn't prepared for Kirk's question. How would Marilou respond?

The pert redhead never hesitated. "I'd scratch her eyes out and teach her respect for other people's property."

"Property! Well, I like that," Bob said, but his face was delighted. "She wasn't kidding, you know. That's just what she'd do. So I'm protected." He turned the tables on Kirk. "Who's going to protect you?"

"Oh, I'll get Kelly here to stand up for me. She can hold her own with any blonde siren, I'm sure!"

Breakfast ended on that note of levity.

43

Kelly went to the cabin for a sombrero, but not before she heard Marilou's low comment to her husband, "She's swell. Maybe she and Kirk can get together."

Bob's comment was equally heartwarming, but a bit more cautious. "She's a thoroughbred, all right, Reddy. But don't try to matchmake. She's been hurt. It shows in her eyes."

"I know. But can you imagine being around Kirk Long and not falling in love with him? He's the nicest man I know." Marilou paused to look into Bob's eyes, her own heart showing. "Except one."

Kelly's face was red as she went on to her cabin, but her heart beat excitedly. This promised to be quite a summer.

And the ride with Kirk was quite a beginning. Never had Kelly seen such scenery, not even in the most exquisitely shot Hollywood films. Great stands of trees, fairly alive with wildlife, both animal and plant. Rabbits with inquisitive eyes. Squirrels and chipmunks that scolded. And always that lofty lady, Mt. Rainier, overlooking them.

"She's like a guardian, a protector," Kelly said. They had stopped to rest their thirsty horses at the edge of the stream where it joined the lake.

"I feel that way, too. I always have. I never

44

stand here without thinking of what the Bible says about man not even being able to imagine how great heaven is. How could anything be more beautiful than this, even heaven?"

Kelly looked at him and sighed in awe. "I never really thought about it." She caught his quick glance. "I guess I have just been too busy."

Kirk nodded. "That's why I wanted to spend my life outdoors. The very meaning of life seems a whole lot clearer when I see what's been done in nature." The horses had finished drinking. "What would you like to do next, Kelly? We've ridden most of the short trails. The mountain will have to wait for another day."

"Believe it or not, I want to go back to camp and eat lunch. I'm starved," she confessed with a laugh, turning her horse around.

"I wouldn't say I told you so for the world, but Mrs. Cunningham did warn you." He glanced at his watch, but made no move to turn his own horse. "Kelly, what do you think of us so far?"

She smiled. "I am unqualifiedly in love with everything. The setting. The food. The people. Aren't the Campbells great? I can't imagine one friend from San Antonio coming right out and saying she was turning down an invitation because she wanted to be alone with her husband! I have a feeling Marilou Campbell and I are going to be good friends. The Cunninghams have already asked me to call them Granny and Gramps. They said it was a term of affection and respect."

Kirk's eyes were teasing. "What else do you like about us, Kelly?" If his unspoken question, *What about me?* reached her, only a heightened color betrayed it.

"I love my horse." She leaned forward, pressed her heels in his sides, and called over her shoulder, "Race you to the house!"

For a moment Kirk stared at her, then reined his horse around. Halfway to the big house he passed her easily, taunting, "Don't try to run away from me, Kelly, it can't be done!"

Her face turned even more scarlet at his words. Was there a hidden meaning? She used the confusion of the ride to hide her own thoughts. The last thing she needed was to get involved with her boss.

"It's so peaceful here." She stretched her arms wide as if to embrace the entire circle of vision. Lunch had left her stuffed and lazy.

"We'll go swimming in an hour or so." Again Kirk grinned at her. "Be prepared. I don't suppose you swim much in lakes."

"Not really. We swim in pools in Texas. But lead on to your lake. Oh, does it have a name?"

"It never had. We always just called it the lake. When I was a kid and after I got back from the hospital, my grandfather really cleaned it up and put in a diving dock, boatlaunching dock, the works. They all had to be repaired, but Gramps has done wonders. We've roped off areas for beginning swimmers and more advanced. Tom Jackson is a qualified lifeguard. Surprisingly enough, so is Lydia. It's her one concession to sports. She's already warned us she won't climb, hike, or ride."

"You really don't like her, do you?" Kelly asked.

Kirk shook his head. "Deep down there's probably a lot of good in her, but I hate what she's doing to her husband. She's like a steamroller, pushing to get what she wants, never satisfied when she does. Maybe this summer will help. I hope so."

"When are they coming?"

"Tomorrow. Lydia wanted to do some extra shopping first."

Why should Kelly feel as if she had been given a reprieve? She had heard so much about Lydia Jackson, she felt as if she had already known her for years!

Yet she wasn't prepared for the way she would meet her. Just outside Kelly's nurse's cabin was a hammock strung between two big trees. The next afternoon Kelly dropped into it, writing materials in hand. She had refused to ride or hike or swim with Kirk.

"I have to write Dr. Lawrence. He will be wondering about my arrival and reactions."

But the soft summer air and gentle breeze were too much for her. The pen dropped from her hand and she slept.

When she awoke, it was with a feeling something was out of place. She opened her eyes. Not five feet away stood a woman — and she *was* out of place. Alpine Meadows had never seen such an outfit, Kelly was sure. It was expensive, lovely, and probably quite fragile. Pale pink from head to toe, even the sandals. Kelly's own crumpled jeans and plaid shirt paled into schoolgirl insignificance beside it. Kelly felt she was also at a disadvantage from being caught asleep.

Why did the intruder's lips narrow into an unfriendly line as she drawled, "You must be the hired nurse."

Kelly couldn't know how beautiful she was, flushed with sleep, dark eyes dewy. For a moment she debated answering in kind but decided against it. "Yes, I'm Kelly Lawr-er,

Lee." She smiled, feeling annoyed at her stuttering and hoping her instant aversion to the woman didn't show.

"I am Lydia Jackson." It was said in a way to demand séervice. Kelly wanted to laugh at the woman's arrogance and pretension. Even one so elegant shouldn't attempt royal manners in Alpine Meadows.

"I see you've met each other." Kirk's voice preceded him. "Hello, Lydia." His tone was cool, his face noncommittal.

Lydia's eyes filled with malice, looking from Kirk to Kelly. "What kind of greeting is that, Kirk" — she drew his face down and kissed him lingeringly — "for a former fiancée?"

"Fiancée!" The unwelcome word slipped past Kelly's lips without her being able to stop it.

"Oh, yes." Lydia's green eyes sharpened. "Didn't Kirk tell you? We were engaged in college, but I refused to marry a man who was going to spend his life with the birds and flowers. Now it seems I'm here anyway. So long, darling." She ran around the edge of the cabin.

"Why didn't you tell me?" Again Kelly could have cut out her tongue. How could she be so gauche?

"Why should I? Believe it or not, that's

one time period I'd just as soon keep buried forever. I must have been out of my mind at the time."

"Now she's here."

"Yes, she is. And I told you why." He looked into her stony face, seeing all her former friendliness hidden by a cloud of doubt. "You can make of it what you like, but all Lydia Jackson is to me is the wife of a good friend."

He turned on his heel and was gone. Even in her state of confusion, Kelly noticed he had gone in the opposite direction from Lydia.

Kelly sank back in the hammock, her brain whirling. Why did the woman have to come and spoil everything? Just when she herself had been ready to believe maybe some men could be true, real men, just as her father had said. Surely, she couldn't trust anyone who could have been attracted to a person as obviously phony as that blonde menace!

"Weren't you attracted to someone like that?" Had she spoken aloud, or was it her subconscious prodding her? She closed her eyes tightly, remembering how her friends had tried to tell her the man who had given her the ring was false. She had flamed with indignation, sure they misunderstood. Until it happened.

She sat up and jumped from the hammock. She wasn't going to lie there in self-pity, remembering things that were best left buried. A passing pang of sympathy for Kirk filled her as she entered her cabin. Was this how he felt? Still, he should have told her.

She never once thought perhaps Kirk would think she should also have told him a thing or two.

What would the summer that had held such promise now bring? The not-too-subtle pursuit of Kirk by his best friend's wife? Kelly shrugged. If he didn't like it, he could put a stop to it.

Yet deep inside was a little disappointment, and as she pulled the hairbrush viciously through her dark hair, she told her reflection, "Just when it seemed like the Garden of Eden around here, enter the snake!"

In spite of herself, the thought tipped up the corner of her mouth on one side. Why should she care? She'd be busy. She wouldn't have much contact with Lydia once the kids came — but that wouldn't be for another week or so.

Kelly was wrong about the arrival of their guests. They started coming earlier than expected. That night during dinner Kirk was called to the phone. When he returned after a long time, he was troubled.

"I'm in something of a spot. You'll all have to help me decide what to do. We aren't completely ready for our guests, but I got a call from a friend in Seattle, a top doctor from Children's Orthopedic Hospital. He has a little boy, about six, who has just come through some pretty extensive surgery to correct some birth defects.

"He's been on a good exercise program, but his parents were killed in a car accident this morning. There's no one there to continue the exercises with him. They can put him back in the hospital, but it doesn't seem wise. The doctor wants to know if we could possibly take David. The boy's distraught."

"It's fine with me," Lydia said. Everyone turned to stare at her. "I'm to work with the older girls, anyway. It won't affect me."

Kelly saw the dislike in the glance Marilou gave the blonde, and she saw the look that passed between Marilou and Bob. "I'll be happy to take David," Marilou said.

"But this was to be a little vacation for you," Kelly protested. "You and Bob were to have some time together."

"It's all right, Kelly. We don't mind if we can help this little boy," Bob said. But he had a cheated look in his eyes.

Kelly decided instantly. "Why can't David stay in the nurse's cabin with me, just until

52

some of the others arrive? I'd be glad to keep him. Then Bob and Marilou can keep their room here and not be split up until later."

"Kelly, you're a winner! That is, if it's okay with you?" Marilou turned to Kirk.

"If Kelly wants to do it this way, that's fine."

"I do. And when you go to get him, Kirk, I'd like to go with you."

"I'll just bet you do." There was mockery in Lydia's voice. "A nice long drive to Seattle with Kirk is enough incentive for anyone to play heroic nurse, isn't it, Miss Lee?"

"Lydia!" Her husband's shocked exclamation was followed by an apologetic look at Kelly.

She had been impressed with the rangy man when she met him earlier. Now she felt sorry for him. He was so obviously in love with his wife, yet equally aware of her bitterness.

"It's all right, Tom." Kelly decided exactly what she should do. She couldn't let the summer turn into a sniping match. Hadn't Kirk said it would be disastrous if there was fighting among the staff? She swallowed hard and smiled at Lydia. "I don't need to pretend for anyone, Lydia. My fiancé is right back in San Antonio waiting for me. We worked at the same hospital before I came here." It was all true, she assured her smarting conscience. He was in San Antonio. He was waiting for her.

"And your ring?" Lydia's eyes bored into Kelly.

"Oh, that." She waved her hand carelessly. "I decided that since I'd be out of doors, away from him and everything, I wouldn't be wearing it." She hadn't known what a capacity for half truth and evasion she had. Marilou and Bob were staring at her, open-mouthed. The Cunninghams had tactfully gone on eating.

Kirk shoved back his chair. "It wasn't necessary for you to explain, Kelly. Thanks for saying you'll take David. I'll make the arrangements to pick him up as soon as we can."

When he had gone, there was silence around the table. Lydia hadn't been prepared for what her probing would reveal. That was evident in the way she crumbled her roll. When she did speak, it was to ask, "Did you say San Antonio, Miss Lee?"

"Yes. That's my hometown."

The meal ended silently, but Marilou walked with Kelly to her cabin. Once they were inside, Marilou closed the door.

"I really appreciate what you're doing for us, Kelly." There was warmth and affection

54

in her smile. "I also appreciate the way you shut up Miss Nosy-Posy. She's a pain in the neck if I ever saw one."

"I feel a little sorry for her."

Marilou gasped. "Sorry for her? Why? I feel sorry for everyone who has to be around her."

Kelly remained firm. "She has everything to make a woman happy. A fine husband, enough money to dress like visiting royalty, beauty, everything. Yet she's miserable inside. I don't know what it would take to make her see she's throwing away the finest thing in the world by lowering herself in Tom's estimation, but that's what she's doing. How long can he keep up that shining-idol image when she acts as she did tonight? When she loses Tom, she'll never get him back."

"I guess you're right. If I acted like that, Bob would either muzzle me or tell me where to get off." She sighed. "I just can't see why Lydia has to be the way she is."

"There are probably a dozen reasons. One thing, I don't want to get a feud started. We have to have peace and joy around these kids that are coming. They've known enough of sorrow and sadness without us inflicting it on them here. How's she going to do with the older girls?"

"Even though I don't like her, I think

she'll be fine," Marilou said. "She's so attractive, the girls should be able to look up to her. It may give her the extra admiration she needs."

"Well." Kelly stretched. "I'm going to try and be friendly, for the sake of Kirk and the kids."

"If you can, I suppose I can, too." Lights danced in Marilou's eyes. "But if she starts hanging around my Bob, there's going to be war!"

Kelly laughed. "I refuse to let one upset woman keep me from enjoying my summer. I love Alpine Meadows and intend to keep on loving it!"

But long after Marilou had gone, Kelly lay in her hammock and thought. What consequences would there be from her statements at the table?

In a large room upstairs in the old log house, Tom Jackson turned his face away from the light.

"Lydia, aren't you ever coming to bed?"

Her blonde hair shone in the light, her green eyes sparkled with mischief.

"I'm almost through. I just remembered I promised to write my cousin. We'll get so busy, there won't be time later."

Her pen flew. Tom dropped off to sleep.

When he awoke, she was still at the big roll-top desk.

"For heavens sake, Lydia! Are you going to write all night?"

"No, dear." There was no endearment in the word, just satisfaction with herself. "I'm on my way."

She licked the stamp, sealed the envelope, and ran with it down to the box that held outgoing mail. Her pale green negligee was thin, slim protection against the cool night air. She shivered as she came back inside from the big rural mailbox.

But inside the mailbox, ready for the morning postman, lay a letter and it was addressed to Lydia's cousin — who just happened to be a staff member of the San Antonio hospital where Kelly had trained and worked.

Chapter 4

Never had Kelly seen a child she didn't love. Even those who came in dirty and unkempt claimed part of her. Yet never had she met a child like David Stewart. She bit her lip to keep from crying as she watched the little boy hobble down the hall to where she and Kirk waited.

"Skinny little chicken, isn't he?" There was a look of compassion in Kirk's eyes. "I bet when we get his shirt off, you can see every bone."

"Not only that." Kelly kept her voice low. "Even through his shirt you can see the way his shoulder blades stick out. I bet he's ten or fifteen pounds underweight."

There was no sparkle in David's eyes when Kirk and Kelly met him. The blue eyes that should have danced with mischief were quiet, acquiescent. His wavy blond hair was almost too neat. There simply wasn't much life to the boy.

"David, you're going to stay with me for a while." Kelly leaned forward eagerly, putting her arm around his unresisting shoulders.

He just looked at her.

"Well, we have quite a drive back to Alpine Meadows," Kirk said. "We'd better be going." He had already stowed David's gear in the station wagon.

He started forward to help the boy, but Kelly motioned him back. David did walk, although awkwardly. He had braces on his legs. In spite of his young age, the little boy had had several operations to correct some birth defects in his legs. The doctor felt confident he would be able to have full use of his legs in time — if his exercises were continued.

"Any restrictions?" Kelly had asked the doctor earlier.

"None at all," the doctor told her. "The more exercise he gets, the better. He also needs daily rubs."

"He'll get them." There was determination in her voice.

David took little interest in the drive to Alpine Meadows. Kelly pointed out the mountain, different trees, including David in her conversation with Kirk, not forcing him to talk.

It wasn't until Kirk slowed the car in almost the same spot where they had seen the deer the day Kelly arrived, that the little boy perked up. The same doe, buck, and two spotted fawns daintily crossed the road.

"Are they real?" This time there was no lack of interest in David's blue eyes.

"They sure are," Kelly said.

"I saw a deer once. I went to a park with my mom and dad —" He fell into silence and a tear fell down his cheek.

"That must have been great," Kirk said. "Now maybe you can see a lot of different animals. Alpine Meadows has squirrels and marmots, chipmunks and rabbits. Even horses." He could feel David's eyes on him. "We even have coyotes that howl in the distance. You know, David, when I was about your age, I used to be scared of those coyotes. My grandpa took me out in the woods one day and we saw a coyote. He looked just like a big dog! The next time I heard one howl, I knew he was just saying, 'Hi, Kirk.' "

"Why did your grandpa take you? Why didn't your dad and mom take you?"

"I didn't have a dad and mom. They died when I was small."

David let out a little sigh and leaned back against the seat. What he was thinking didn't show, but Kelly and Kirk guessed it would be of his parents.

A little later, his ridiculously long lashes fell to his cheeks and David slept. Kelly drew him in the circle of her arms.

"What will happen to him? After he leaves us, I mean?"

Kirk's lips were set in a straight line. "He isn't going to be leaving."

"What do you mean?"

"He doesn't have a place to go. It would be an orphanage for him. I told the doctor to check into what it would take for adoption."

"Adoption!"

"Certainly. If David comes to love Alpine Meadows, and I think he will, he's going to get to stay there."

"Do they let single men adopt?"

"Sometimes. If not, I suppose I could get a wife — somewhere. Too bad you're already engaged, in spite of what you told me the day we met." He ignored her murmur and went on smoothly. "You would have been quite perfect for the job. As David's mother, of course."

Before she could think of a protest strong enough to scorch this arrogant creature, he swung into Alpine. "Better get gas." The subject of marriage was clearly closed.

"Wake up, David, we're home," Kelly said a short time later. Curious, her feelings as she lifted the little boy.

"I'm not even going to undress him," she

told Kirk. "He needs all the rest he can get. He's been emotionally battered until he's had about all he can take."

"Poor little picked chicken." There was no trace of mockery in Kirk's voice, only sympathy.

But when David was tucked in, Kirk turned to Kelly. "If you decide to leave that engagement ring off permanently, maybe we could work something out. Good night."

The door closed behind him, leaving Kelly frustrated. What did a person do with a man like Kirk Long? He had as many facets as a chameleon. Well, at least the summer wouldn't be boring!

No one was surprised when David began to relax and accept the Cunninghams, then Marilou and Bob Campbell. Everyone *was* surprised with what developed between David and Lydia. The first time he saw her, he went to her.

"Pretty lady." He touched her blonde hair. "Mama?"

For a moment the usually cynical face didn't move. Then a smile crossed Lydia's features and she held out her arms. "Come here, David."

From that moment on, they were inseparable during the day. At night David obediently slept in the nurse's cabin, but he spent as much time as he could with Lydia.

"I sure wouldn't have expected it of her," Marilou confided in Kelly. "She seems to adore the kid. I wouldn't have thought she would ever like kids. You notice they don't have any."

Kelly had been giving it thought. "You know, Marilou, maybe she can't have children. It would explain a lot — her frantic pushing Tom to get her fancy clothes and so on. She might feel she's failed him, so she flirts with all the other men to show him how desirable she is."

Neither of them had heard the soft footsteps on the trail. At a choking sound, they turned to face a blazing-eyed Lydia.

"And suppose I can't have kids?" the blonde snapped. "What business is it of yours? What are you, some kind of amateur psychologist? I'll thank you to keep your long nose out of my business, Kelly Lee." She turned to Marilou. "That goes double for you."

Marilou's red hair and temper to match exploded. "Are you naturally nasty, Lydia, or do you practice it? So we were discussing you. Actually, we were glad you've taken over so much care of David, helping him with swimming and stuff. You should eavesdrop on an entire conversation if you're go-

ing to listen at all. It might make a big difference in the way you see yourself!"

Without a word, Lydia turned on her heel
and left. Kelly was shaken. The unpleasant
incident had no place in Alpine Meadows.
Thank goodness, David hadn't been there to
hear it.

"We really were in the wrong, talking
about her," Kelly said, feeling miserable over
the whole thing.

"Maybe so. All I know is that Lydia's a
pill. I'd bet David's mother was a blonde or
he ought to know better than to like Lydia."
Marilou made a wry face. "That's a rotten
thing to say. When she's cooled down, I'll
apologize."

Kelly shook her head. "I think you should
keep still, and me, too. The less said about
it, the better. The more we talk of it, the
more trouble there'll be. Let it die naturally."

Marilou finally agreed, rather reluctantly,
then said, "I can't promise not to scratch
back if she ruffles my fur!"

"One more day!" Bob Campbell finished
his dinner coffee and grinned. "Do you folks
realize this is our last day of peace and
quiet?"

"Come on, Bob, the kids are coming one

64

at a time, not all in a bunch," Marilou said.

"Wonder how we're going to like being dorm mommies and daddies?" Bob was determined to dig a little. "I've had such a good time the last few days, I almost forgot I was going to work this summer, not play."

"Work!" Marilou grinned. "Some work — riding and hiking and all those fun things." She appealed to Kelly. "Do you call it work, what we'll be doing?"

"Only if we get broken bones and all that." Kelly refused to be baited. "Actually, I can't think of a more beautiful place to be than right here."

"Not even in San Antonio with your fiancé?" Lydia couldn't keep out of the conversation.

"Not even in San Antonio with my fiancé." Kelly smiled, stood, and walked to the door. There was no sense in answering Lydia and creating a rift in the armed truce between them.

"Why don't we have a campfire tonight?" Kirk suggested, coming up behind Kelly. "There's going to be a moon." He looked down at David, who was tugging on his arm. "How about a campfire, David?"

"Sure!" The face framing those blue eyes was no longer so thin and pale. The hours outdoors with Lydia had begun their work.

For the umpteenth time Kelly vowed she wouldn't let Lydia get under her skin again. If she didn't do anything all summer except help David, she still would have done her part.

The campfire was a great success. David was intrigued when Bob suggested they make smores.

"What's a smore?" the boy demanded, watching Bob prepare one.

"It's a graham cracker with a piece of chocolate and a toasted marshmallow all gooey and running over it."

"But why's it called a smore?"

Bob popped the delicious morsel in David's open mouth. " 'Cause it's so good that when you eat one you say 'I want s'more!' "

Even Lydia relaxed and laughed at Bob's nonsense.

From seemingly out of nowhere, Tom pulled out a guitar and strummed.

"I didn't know you played a guitar, Tom!" Lydia's hand was poised midair with her smore.

"There are a lot of things you don't know about me, Lydia." As if touched by her interest, he dropped his usual quiet attitude and began to clown.

David sat wide-eyed and grinning as Tom

66

sang song after crazy song for his benefit. One was about a skunk, another about a fat lady sitting on someone's hat. Kelly and the others were speechless with laughter when he finally bowed and stopped.

"Let's all sing," he suggested.

The fire had died to a mere flicker. The moon had risen over the lake, making things eerily bright.

Kelly would never forget that special night. For once there was no bickering, just the joy of people singing together around a campfire. They started with "Home on the Range," which was followed by songs like "Bicycle Built for Two" and "The Bear Went Over the Mountain."

"You know who's just been appointed songleader," Kirk told Tom. "I've been wondering if I was going to have to do it myself." He lowered his voice to bullfrog depth. "I sing in the basement."

Not to be outdone, irrepressible Marilou added, "When I was small, I was sent to an Italian singing teacher. She listened to me and said, 'Some people, they singa on the white notes. Some people, they singa on the black notes. But you? You singa in the cracks.' It was the end of my singing career!"

But in spite of the laughter, David's eyelids were drooping.

"We better get him back to bed," Kelly suggested and stood.

"I'll take him," Lydia said. Then she just walked up the trail with David in her arms.

Tom looked after her with troubled eyes. Kirk and the Cunninghams and Campbells were putting out the fire, gathering wrappers and trash to take back to camp.

"I think she finds something in David she'd never had before," Kelly impulsively said to Tom.

"Will you walk home with me?" Tom seemed a bit hesitant. "I've been wanting to talk with you."

"I'd love to." They moved onto the trail Lydia had taken.

"I don't know what Kirk has told you," Tom said. "Anyway, Lydia and I are at a crossroads. Our marriage isn't really a marriage. It's just two people who share the same building, the same apartment. I don't know what it is she wants. I feel I've failed her."

Sighing, Kelly asked, "Tom, I know this is personal, but is Lydia unable to have children?"

"Yes, she is." He looked surprised. "Why do you ask?"

"Because one day Marilou and I were talking and she heard us." Kelly told Tom what had happened. "She was furious, but I could see that what we'd said might have hurt her deeply." They walked on in silence. "Maybe she feels she has failed you by not giving you a child."

Tom was quiet so long, Kelly wondered if he planned to answer. "You might be right. All this mad rush to have the best clothes and things — even when she got them, she wasn't happy. But what can I do?"

They had reached the clearing and Kelly's cabin. "I think David is doing a great deal of it for you, Tom."

"But what about when the summer's over, when she has to give him up?"

A wild thought dashed through Kelly's brain. "Does she have to do that?"

"What do you mean?"

"Kirk is already checking into adoption. He doesn't know if it can be approved, a single man. But what if —" Kelly's imagination caught fire — "you and Lydia adopted David?"

"Adopted David?"

"Why not? Lydia seems to worship him and he follows her everywhere. Why don't you just hold off, watch what happens, and keep it in mind?"

Impulsively Tom caught her hand. "Kelly, you may have just solved all my problems.

You're a darling!"

She was amazed when the tall, quiet man leaned down and kissed her on the cheek.

He jerked back when an icy voice cut in, "Miss Lee seems to have an amazing capacity for problem-solving, or is it just plain interference?"

Not waiting for an answer, Lydia tucked her arm through Tom's. "Thank you so much for consoling my husband, Miss Lee, but in the future I can assure you it will be unnecessary. Neither of us need your meddling. Any problems we might have will be taken care of without outside parties butting in."

She pulled Tom after her and disappeared down the trail to the main log house.

"What was that all about?" Kirk loomed dark and stern in the path.

"Nothing, absolutely nothing!" Kelly's breath was coming in furious little pants. "I told Tom I thought Lydia might want to adopt David. She seems to love and need him so much, it would be hard for them to be separated at the end of the summer. I told him you didn't know if they'd let you have him because you were single. He was grateful and kissed me."

Steel fingers bit into Kelly's arms. "So he was grateful and kissed you. I see."

Something in his face gleamed in the moon-light and Kelly shrank a little in his tight clutch. "Well, Miss Kelly Lee, I am also grateful, very grateful. So . . ." The moon and stars were blotted out by his head. Kirk Long leaned down and kissed Kelly full on the lips.

"You — you —" She wrenched herself free. "How dare you!"

His face was enigmatic in the moonlight. "To use an old cliché, the more the merrier. If you want to play insulted maiden, you can slap me." He turned his lean brown face sideways.

For one moment Kelly was tempted to do exactly that. Not for anything would she ad-mit even to herself that the kiss he had given her had stirred something deep within her. It had been so gentle, yet so warm, so excit-ing, so unlike the way she had ever been kissed before.

Her lips curved in scorn. "I wouldn't lower myself to your level, caveman."

Her shot scored. Even in the moonlight, she could see Kirk's pose drop. "Caveman? Maybe you'd like to see what a caveman really is."

He took one purposeful step toward her. It was enough for Kelly. Her dignity dropped and she ran for her cabin like a frightened

71

rabbit. But she couldn't run away from his laughter, ringing out over the moonlit night, swelling into echoing gales against the distant hills.

I hate him, she told herself furiously, pounding her fists into an imaginary assailant, yet being careful not to awaken David.

Yet long after her lights were out, Kelly lay awake, thinking over the strange evening with all its implications.

It wasn't until she awoke the next morning that she realized for the first time she could think of San Antonio and her former fiancé without a pang.

"I'm free!" She spoke out loud.

A sleepy David poked his head around the corner and she beckoned him into bed with her. "Come on, David. Today's the day we start getting other guests. You're an old-timer here now. You'll have to make the other kids feel at home. Okay?"

His lips were set with six-year-old responsibility. "Sure, Kelly. What do I do?"

She snuggled the warm little body starting to fill out next to her. "What do you think you can do?"

"Well." The eyes got big. "I can show them Granny and Gramps. I can tell them not to get near the horses. I can bring them here if they fall down." He thought hard.

72

"And I can let them use Mama Lydia if they're lonesome."

Kelly hugged him hard. "You can do all that, David. Good for you. Now let's get your legs rubbed and get dressed for the day."

Even in the short time David had been with them, the sun and good food and constant care were beginning to pay off. Kelly rubbed his legs daily. He swam and ran and played.

Kelly hadn't said anything to him, but when he went back to the orthopedic surgeon for his next checkup, she hoped he could have the braces removed. What a day it would be — for all of them.

This time Kelly didn't go to Seattle with Kirk to pick up their guests. She had prepared a casual, "I think I'll stay here," to answer his request.

He hadn't requested. He'd simply said, "Bob, mind if I borrow Marilou today? She can ride in with me to get the kids. The rest of you will be busy getting ready, I'm sure. We're bringing out two girls and a boy, all teenagers."

Bob had agreed, but Kelly had looked up in time to see Kirk tossing a smile in her direction. It had infuriated her, but she'd made a point of being on hand when Bob waved them off. She had even called, "Have a good trip!"

Not for anything would she have the conceited oaf think she cared whether he asked her or not! Besides, as he had said, there was plenty to be done.

"Where am I going to stay now?" David looked a little woebegone when Kelly started packing his gear.

"You'll be in with Bob. You like him, don't you?"

"Sure. But I like you, too." His grin was delightful.

One tooth had recently fallen out and a dime had been found under his pillow. He was beginning to look more like a regular little boy than a wraith.

"I like you a lot, too, David. But your bed will be used for the children who get sick or hurt. We hope no one does. But we have to be prepared."

"How come I got to stay here?" He grinned again. " 'Cause I'm special?"

"Very special." Kelly hugged him hard. "Besides, the dorms haven't been opened until today."

"Okay. I'll stay with Bob." He paused on the doorstep. "But I'm coming back to see you, anyway!"

One more grin and he was gone, leaving a

misty-eyed nurse blinking back tears. A few short days at Alpine Meadows had wrought such changes in David. She hoped the place would do the same for all the others who would come.

Chapter 5

"Whew!" Marilou mopped her hot face, pushing the red curls off her forehead. "Did you ever try to fit three teenagers, all their stuff, one driver, and one frazzled woman into a station wagon?"

Kelly laughed. "That bad, huh?"

"Not really." Marilou made a face. "I'm just griping a little when I shouldn't." Her eyes grew sober. "Kelly, how do you stand being a children's nurse?"

"I love it. Why?"

Marilou put her hand over the general region of her heart. "I feel funny in here when I see these kids, so brave, needing help so much but not wanting to take it. I don't think I could stand working with the ones who aren't making it."

"I understand." A meaningful look passed between them. "You never get used to it. You have to feel the ones you help outweigh those who won't get well — ever."

A little pool of silence fell, broken only by the soft wind in the trees near the nurse's cabin. Marilou had managed to slip away for a few minutes before supper to tell Kelly of the trip to Seattle. Both girls were sitting on the grass near the hammock.

"Marilou, what are you and Bob going to do when summer is over?" Kelly suddenly asked.

"I don't know. Whatever Bob wants." She colored. "I suppose that sounds terribly old-fashioned and everything, but it really isn't. Whatever makes him happy will satisfy me."

"You're really a wonderful person, you know?"

Marilou smiled. "Who me? Not really. I just happen to love Bob."

"Glad to hear it." Bob's wide grin as he came around the cabin displayed his delight. "Caught you talking about me, didn't I, woman?" He rumpled her red curls as he sat down. "Move over, wife, and let a tired interior decorator rest."

"Interior decorator. Oh, sure, moving beds and stuff."

"A lot more than that." He clasped one of Marilou's hands. "Lydia has a good idea about changing some of the arrangements. You'll find out at a staff meeting after supper." He let go of Marilou's hand and stood up, his eyes dancing. "No, I won't tell you now. You have to wait."

★ ★ ★

Supper was over. The three new guests were on the long porch with David. He was taking his new responsibilities seriously. Surprisingly, the teenagers were listening, paying attention as he told them where things were.

Kelly couldn't remember last names but knew the two boys were named Sam and Dean, and the girl was Susan. She was watching them through the dining-room window. Her wandering thoughts were snapped to attention by Kirk's entering the room.

"We want to talk something over. Lydia has come up with a plan that sounds better than what we had in mind and we want to get your reaction." Kirk paused and looked around the circle.

"Now that we're starting to get our guests, it'll be a different situation. Everything will be done for their benefit, not our own. Yet there's no reason we can't make things easier on ourselves, too. I had originally asked you to split up, with Lydia and Marilou taking the girls in one dorm, and Bob and Tom taking the boys. Then, also, everyone would have his or her own age group of kids all the time. It would mean not much time off for any of you. The only time you'd be free is when Kelly and I could relieve you."

He turned to the blonde counselor. "Lydia, I'm going to ask you to tell the group what you suggested."

For the first time Lydia's face was alight with something other than vanity. "I was just wondering if it wouldn't work out better to split up on a more family-like basis. The younger kids especially will need a lot of loving care. At least until we get too many, couldn't we just take turns assigning them? Those dorms have separate rooms for two or three single beds. How would it work if Tom and I took one cabin, and Bob and Marilou the other? And then every other guest would be assigned to a 'family unit' instead of by age and sex."

She hesitated and looked at Tom. "That would give us husband and wife teams a chance to be together more, too — in a family situation." Kelly caught the longing in her eyes and voice.

"Well, what do you think? Bob?" Kirk asked.

"I'm all for it. Anything that will give me more time with Reddy!" He was greeted by a shout of laughter, but he held firm. "I'm not kidding. Besides, I think it would be great for the kids. Those partitions aren't all that hard to take down where you were going to separate by age. We'd have one large living space, with our sleeping rooms private. Marilou and I would be right there on call all the time, just like when we have a family."

"Marilou?" Kirk said.

Her sparkling eyes and wide grin answered for her. "Lydia, you're a jewel!" She didn't even notice the pleased look on the blonde woman's face. "If I were a kid trying to recuperate, it would be nice to feel I had a family setup."

"Tom?"

"I'm not sure." Lydia's face fell but brightened as her husband explained. "I like your idea, Lydia, but I don't know about this every-other-one business. Seems it would be better to keep the boys with one couple and the girls with the other. For instance, suppose David's assigned with two teenage girls. Or we get one teenage girl with a bunch of little boys. Why not let us take the boys, and Bob and Marilou can have the girls?"

"Okay with you, Bob and Marilou?" Kirk asked.

"Sure," Marilou said. "David's so crazy over Lydia, he shouldn't be taken from her." Again her praise seemed to help thaw Lydia.

Kirk turned to the Cunninghams. "I know you aren't personally involved, but what do you think of the idea?"

"It's a good one," Gramps said. "I think

the kids and you would be better off."

Granny seconded Gramps. "Also, if Bob and Marilou or Tom and Lydia would like to get away for a night or two, we could move in and substitute for them."

Lydia jumped up. "Oh, I didn't mean for you to have to leave your work. With a cabin full of kids, who needs to get away?"

"Thanks, Lydia. I appreciate that." Kirk's smile was singularly sweet. "Just one more to hear from. Kelly, what's your feeling on it? You work with kids all the time. Do you think this is a good idea?"

Kelly was still trying to adjust to this new image of Lydia. She was so pleased by the blonde's constructive attitude and helpful suggestion that she didn't know what to say. "Well, I don't know —" Kelly began.

The words were misunderstood.

Lydia turned on her furiously. "No, you wouldn't. You wouldn't know anything! Any nurse who would give the patient the wrong medicine and hide behind the fact her father was chief of staff at a hospital —"

"Lydia!" Tom thundered.

For a moment his tone seemed to cow her. Then she jerked free from her husband's hand. Kelly could see fingerprints in her flesh where he had grabbed her.

"I don't care," Lydia said vindictively. "It's

81

true. My own cousin works in that Texas hospital. She said if it had been anyone but the chief's daughter, she'd have been thrown out. That's probably why she got sent out here. She's even ashamed to use her own name! She isn't Kelly Lee. She's Kelly Lawrence!"

If the earth had opened at that moment, Kelly would have crawled into it and disappeared. The circle of faces was indelibly impressed on her memory. Until time ended, she'd remember each one.

Bob and Marilou were angry. The Cunninghams looked a little sick at the distasteful scene. Tom was white to the lips, futilely trying to shut up the triumphant Lydia, who had changed from an eager, interested woman into a vicious shrew in the space of moments.

And Kirk's face. Looking at him, Kelly bit her lip until it bled. His face was gray. He started to speak but was cut off by Lydia's shrill voice.

"Say it isn't true, Kelly Lawrence — if you dare. You don't. Everyone knows about it at the hospital in San Antonio. Everyone also knows how you were engaged to Brad Harrington, one of the top doctors there — and how he jilted you over this whole mess!"

"No one jilted Kelly!" Marilou snapped,

jumping into the battle. "She's engaged."

"Oh, no, she's not! That's another lie, along with Lee, the cooked-up name."

"Kelly?" Marilou turned toward her friend, but Kirk finally got into the act.

"That's enough!" His voice cracked like a dead tree in a lightning storm. "There will be no further discussion of this! Whether Kelly is Lee or Lawrence is immaterial.

"What happened at her hospital is also immaterial. She was highly recommended by Dr. Lawrence, who is a nationally respected children's orthopedic surgeon. He wouldn't send us anyone, not even his daughter, who wasn't highly competent. Now if there's nothing else for the staff to discuss that relates to Alpine Meadows" — he underlined the words with his voice and a pointed look at Lydia — "I suggest we get back to whatever needs to be done. For tonight we'll get our guests housed temporarily. Tomorrow we'll get those partitions down. Meeting over."

They stood, not looking at Kelly, then were stopped by Kirk's curt command. "One thing more. There will be no further talk about this among any of you. If I find that rule broken, out you go. Period."

In numbed silence Kelly watched them go. Granny Cunningham patted her on the shoulder as she passed.

"Sorry, child. Don't worry about it. When someone's full of poison like a rattlesnake, they just naturally have to bite someone else or die from their own venom. Lydia's like that, filled with hate and bitterness. If you can't forgive her, at least pity her." Another pat and she was gone.

"Kelly?" Kirk dropped into the chair across from her. "Do you want to talk about it?"

"There's nothing to say." Her voice was dull. "I'll start packing right away."

"Packing! We won't be going camping for another week at least."

"You mean I'm not to leave Alpine Meadows?"

"No, Kelly. We need you." For one moment he put his big, warm hand over hers. "I would have preferred it if you didn't lie to me about who you were." He cut off her involuntary protest. "You must have had a good reason. Just one question — are you engaged?"

"No."

With an agile leap he bounded for the door. "Good, Kelly." He stopped and said something Kelly didn't catch, then waved and was gone, leaving Kelly on the verge of tears.

Slowly she walked from the big log house, avoiding the front where the guests were gathered, avoiding the clearing and the dormitories. If only she could crawl to her cabin like a wounded fox to his den!

Maybe in the peace and privacy she could overcome the emotions Lydia had forced to the surface. She had thought them buried, but in one moment the wild slashing of Lydia's tongue had let loose a Pandora's box of troubles. She needed privacy.

No, not the cabin, Kelly thought. Someone might come. Surely it wouldn't matter if she walked to the lake. Everyone was busy. Kirk had a cardinal rule that staff members must be accounted for at all times, in case they were needed. But there wasn't much chance for an accident now. There wasn't much chance she would be needed.

Kelly headed for the lake trail. First she had walked and ridden it with Kirk. She couldn't think of him without crying. His disappointment in her over what he considered lying had mingled with enough faith and trust to keep her on. Was it because of her father?

She had come here under an assumed name to make it on her own. Now perhaps she was only being retained because she was Dr. Lawrence's daughter!

She was tasting the dregs of misery. The lake blurred from her sight. The moon rose. An owl hooted, hesitated, and was answered by a more distant hoot. A bush swayed at the brushing of an animal's body and was still. A deer had come to drink. It eyed the motionless figure of the girl, decided she was harmless, and bent down at the water's edge.

Kelly heard and saw none of it. She was too engrossed in her own thoughts. Maybe she should leave, in spite of what Kirk had said. But if she did, what would he do for medical help? That thought added pounds of weight to her chains of helplessness.

She was needed here. She would have to stay, to see Lydia's mocking smile, the doubt in the Campbells' faces. Her shoulders shook. How could she ever have gotten in this situation?

From the past came a stark scene at the bedside of a dying patient.

"The wrong medicine? Impossible!" a white-faced doctor exclaimed.

Kelly worked feverishly beside him to no avail. She sighed heavily at the final drawing of a sheet over the wasted frame.

Again, in her mind's eye, Kelly stumbled from the room, felt the grip of fingers digging into her shoulders.

She jumped to her feet, tried to run, and realized the grip was no nightmare of the past. She was being gripped and a voice was demanding, just as it had that night at the hospital, "Where do you think you're going?"

Kirk! She sagged with relief, frantically freeing herself from the past. "Oh, it's you!"

The fingers did not relax. Would there be bruises there tomorrow?

"What are you trying to pull? You know the number one rule around here is to be on duty. While you've been sitting down here drowning your own troubles in the lake, we've had an accident — and no nurse!"

"Oh, no! Not David?"

"Not David. Mrs. Cunningham dropped a pan of hot water and burned her arm. Fortunately, Marilou's first aid was all that was needed. It wasn't serious. But it could have been!"

"I'm sorry." Kelly felt like a small schoolgirl being reprimanded by the principal.

Kirk loosened his grip and pointed to a rock in the moonlight. "Sit down, Kelly." He no longer sounded angry, just tired. "I didn't think I'd have to talk to you the way I did to the Campbells and Jacksons. Evidently I was wrong. You should know that when you're working with patients, and this once

I will refer to them as such, you have no place in your life for personal problems.

"I don't know what happened in San Antonio and I don't want to know. You're needed here. You have the skills to help these kids. Now get rid of whatever it is that's holding you back. In your condition, you're worse than useless."

Kelly's heart felt cut to ribbons. If he had yelled or stormed around, it would have been worse. Yet the disappointment in his voice, the truth of his statements, cut her to pieces.

"You have tonight to think things through. You know you're needed here." He looked at the bent head and softened. "And wanted. We have four youngsters now who will be needing you. And we have more than a dozen coming. It's up to you, but I want to know tomorrow morning if you can put aside your own life, and work for the sake of others — at least for this summer."

The doubt in his voice stung Kelly to action as nothing else could have done. "I don't need until tomorrow morning." She got up from the rock and looked him full in the face. "I know I overreacted to Lydia and shouldn't have. What's past is past. Starting tomorrow I'm Kelly Lee Lawrence, R.N. As such, I'll be what you expected from my recommendation."

"So your name really is Kelly Lee." He waited for her to precede him on the path. "You didn't lie about that."

"No. I — I just left out the last part."

The sounds of breaking brush attested to the night life abroad. Kelly was glad for Kirk's company on the trail. She still wasn't used to the noises of mountain nights. When they reached the cabin, he stopped her.

"Kelly, don't think I'm unsympathetic to you and your problems. Even though I knew afterward I'd escaped a lot of misery, when Lydia broke our engagement, I thought the world would end. I know you must have loved Dr. Harrington a great deal." His voice was husky. "Don't let it turn you against life — or other men."

Kelly stared after him as he strode across the clearing, his shadow in the moonlight ten feet tall. Who would have suspected Kirk Long of such perception? She shivered as she entered the cabin. Even a summer night by a lake in the mountains required a jacket, and she had been too upset to grab one when she left.

But she had other things to think about. Waves of shame scorched her at the thought she had been absent when needed. AWOL. Just like a soldier who had run from duty. It took her a long time to get warm enough to prepare for bed. When she crawled in, she was shocked to see an envelope pinned to her pillow.

Kelly's blood congealed. Was it a poison pen letter from Lydia? She picked it up between the tips of her fingers and threw it in the wastebasket unopened. Turning out the light, she closed her eyes. Mentally, she could still picture that envelope. Plain, white — it really hadn't looked like Lydia. She sighed, turned the light back on, reached for the envelope, and opened it. Then she read the enclosed note.

Dear Kelly,

Kirk said we couldn't talk about what happened tonight. He didn't say we couldn't write letters about it.

Bob and I just want you to know that whatever it is that's bothering you, we're on your side. We've learned to love you as a sister even in the short time we've been at Alpine Meadows. The shadow in your eyes when you came has been disappearing and we were glad. Don't let this throw you.

As for Lydia — well, the funniest thing happened. Even when she was acting so rotten, all I could think of was what you said that day about her not having anything when Tom lost the scales from his eyes and saw her as she was. (My words, not yours.) Tonight I think that happened. I've never seen him look like he did.

Just wanted to let you know we're all for you, Kelly.

Love,
Marilou

P.S. We don't think you gave any wrong medicine, either, no matter what anyone says!!

Kelly's eyes stung. What wonderful, loyal friends! They didn't even ask for explanations, just accepted her as she was. She reread the letter, then carefully tore it to bits. She didn't need it. Its message of cheer and faith in her had sunk deep into her heart.

In the darkness, as the chill night air blew across her face, Kelly faced the thought of Lydia. Also, snatches of what had been communicated to her earlier came back to her in those moments of never-never land between waking and sleeping.

Granny: "If you can't forgive . . . pity."

Marilou: "I've never seen Tom look like he did tonight."

Kirk: "I thought the world would end. . . .
You must have loved Dr. Harrington a great
deal."

That was it, the key. Even in her practically
sleeping state, Kelly knew she had hold of
the key, the tense Kirk had used, "must have
loved."

The last thing she heard before the night
wind finally claimed her in sleep was her own
voice saying, "What's past is past. I'm Kelly
Lee Lawrence, R.N."

She struggled desperately to hold onto
that. When tomorrow came, she would need
the assurance that had come to her tonight.

Chapter 6

"Kelly, I wish you'd talk with Susan." Marilou's usually sunny face was clouded. "Something's bothering her and I can't seem to get through." She sighed. "Much as I love my 'family,' they are really a preview of what mothers actually go through! I think I worry more over these kids than I do Bob."

"Impossible."

Marilou perked up at the laughter in Kelly's voice. "Okay, so I'm always showing how I feel about my man. Is that bad?"

"No, it isn't." Kelly moved to the edge of her porch and gazed off into the forest with unseeing eyes. "I wish Lydia were more like you."

"Is she giving you trouble?"

"No. She's kept out of my way since the explosion. It's just that I see her trying to show her feelings toward Tom and not being able to. Maybe she's held back so long, it isn't natural to her."

"She's doing a good job with her 'family' of boys." Marilou stretched and yawned. "I heard one of them telling Gramps Cunningham living with the other boys and the Jacksons was more of a home than he'd ever had."

"Was that Sam, the boy from the broken home?"

"No." Marilou's face turned serious again. "It was Dean."

"But he should have everything going for him!" Kelly protested. "They're certainly affluent enough."

"Too much so. I guess the father's so busy making a living to keep them in the style they want, he never has time to do anything with Dean. And it's never easy being an only child, you know that. When your dad's too busy, it's even worse."

Kelly sank back into her chair. "That's one of the hazards of working with children and teens, Marilou. With all patients, come to think of it. You not only heal their bodies, you have to work with their spirits."

"I know. Even when I want to cry, I can see the results. Can you believe it's been six weeks since we started getting guests? Our family has grown to ten, and the Jacksons have eight. I asked if we were going to have to stop taking them, but Kirk reminded me some of the first ones are ready to go home."

Marilou stopped, put a finger to her lips

and considered. "Kelly, I have a hunch about Susan — no! I want you to talk with her and see what you think."

Later that afternoon Kelly saw Susan crossing the field. She walked with a free stride. Little remained of the limp she had had when she arrived. Long hours in the sun, hiking, riding, had done their work. Her problem had been slight compared to some of the others. Now she was ready to go home.

Susan looked up and saw Kelly. The strangest thing happened. Her limp grew more pronounced. The springy stride slackened. By the time she got to the porch, she was panting.

"Marilou said you wanted to see me."

"I'm just a little lonely, Susan. You've progressed until you haven't needed me for quite a while." Kelly smiled at the pretty brown-haired girl. "You're ready to be discharged. I'll need to give you a final checkup before sending you back to your own doctor for a clean record."

"I'm not going." The teenager spoke flatly with no attempt at courtesy.

"But, Susan! You've done wonderfully up here. It's time for you to get back to your friends, and —"

"What friends?" Susan's scowl obliterated

her prettiness. "Everyone back home hates me."

"Susan!"

"It's true." She pounded the porch railing. "My brother and sister both resent my having to have the operation. It took money they needed for other things. They feel I'm the petted and spoiled one. Besides, why should I go back? They don't even think I'm normal."

Kelly drew back from the girl's bitterness. Her voice was gentle. "Would you like to talk about it?"

"No — yes — I don't know. Oh, sure, why not? About a year ago, I was in an accident. My leg was twisted pretty badly. The first operation helped a lot, but I limped. My family called me 'gimpy' and said I'd be a cripple, a burden. They never wanted me to start with. Mom said I was a mistake. They hadn't planned for other children — then I arrived."

Kelly flinched from the pain in the girl's voice. How many times parents told their children they had been afterthoughts. Why didn't they realize what they were doing to them?

"I'm sure they love you, Susan."

"Not much. If I go home, I'll have to face all of them. I just can't do it." Without warning, she burst into hysterical sobs. "Do you know what it's like, Kelly, to want someone to love you and know they don't? Do you know how it feels to be the mistake, the one your family didn't want? Have you ever been so hurt it would have been easier to be dead?"

Intuition flashed through Kelly. What she said now could affect Susan's life forever. "Yes, Susan. I have felt left out, unwanted. Not because of brothers and sisters. Because I didn't have any brothers and sisters. My mother died and Dad raised me." She swallowed hard. "He's the greatest. But there was a lot of lonely time."

Susan looked up, touched by something in Kelly's voice. "Lonely time?"

"You know. Like when I'd see other families together on picnics, or in the park. Most of the time Dad was too busy working to be with me. When he was, it was great. He did his best. But he couldn't totally take the place of a mother and brothers and sisters. I used to say when I grew up I was going to have a half dozen kids so none of them would ever be lonely."

Something stirred in the depths of the younger girl's tear-filled eyes. "Gee, Kelly, I never thought of it that way. We fight so much in our family I always wished I'd

97

been an only child."

Kelly patted the girl's arm. "We always wish we were something different from what we are. Susan, deep down, would you really want to trade off your family?"

Susan stared ahead of her for a long time. "I don't know. Maybe not. I guess I should think about it."

"Would you like me to write your mother? Find out about the arrangements for taking you home?"

Susan's shoulders slumped. "I suppose so. I can't stay here forever. If only I could!"

"I don't want to preach, Susan. But running away doesn't help anything."

A flash of insight caught Kelly's breath. Wasn't that just what she herself had done? Run away? Slipped off from an unpleasant situation?

But that had been different. *Had it?* her conscience asked. She impatiently brushed the question away.

Susan was the important one right now; her own problems could wait. Kirk had been right. Personal problems could not be allowed to come between the needs of the young people and her ability to give.

"If only I knew they really wanted me!"

Susan's cry haunted Kelly for the next few hours. Even though she had walked away, strong and apparently well, Kelly knew the girl was not healed inside where it mattered. Could she do anything? How could she approach the subject with Susan's family?

She didn't have to. Sunday was visiting day at Alpine Meadows. The first arrivals came in a bunch, a station wagon full of people. A mother, father, and five assorted children.

The youngest faced Kelly accusingly. "Where's Aunt Susan?"

"Aunt Susan?" Kelly felt bewildered.

"Sure. Oh, there she is!" He raced across the grounds to Susan, who was heading toward him. The others followed the child. Kelly had never seen such joy on a human being's face as there was on Susan's.

"Jim, Mike, Debbie — you came!"

"Of course, we came! Think we could forget you?"

"But I've been here six weeks, and it's so far from Bellingham, and gas is so expensive, and —"

"And we miss you terribly, Susan." A brown-haired girl a little older than Susan hugged her. She must be the one Susan had called Debbie. "I never thought I'd be so lonely in that room of ours with you gone, but it's been awful!"

"Mom?"

Kelly closed her eyes in a little prayer. Let the mother say the right thing.

"I'm so glad you're well! Why, your limp is gone, Susan. We're proud of you, honey." The woman, a slightly faded edition of Susan and Debbie, turned to Kelly. "You know, I've always had to hold back to keep from spoiling her rotten since she's my youngest."

There was great love in the mother look she gave Susan. Kelly saw Susan open up like a sunflower to the sun. One short sentence had blotted out the hurt and misunderstanding of years.

"Aunt Susan, can we see where you live?" It was the young boy who had demanded to know where Susan was.

"Sure, I'll show you around. But first" — her eyes were proud, her head high — "I want you to meet my friend, Kelly Lawrence. She's our Alpine Meadows nurse."

There was thankfulness in Susan's face. "She really helped me a lot." A look of total understanding passed between them as Susan introduced her parents, sister, older brother and wife, and their two boys.

"When do you get to come home?" her mother asked.

"Well." Susan hesitated, then turned to Kelly, eyes sparkling. "Can I go today?"

"If you'll take time for me to give you the once-over. You'll have to see your own doctor when you get home."

"She will." The father spoke for the first time. "We can't spare her any longer than necessary, but we want to make sure she's whole."

"I think you'll find she's more whole than ever before in her life."

Only Susan grasped the full meaning of Kelly's words. Before she could do more than smile, Mike and Jim had her by the arms.

"Come on, Aunt Susan. Show us the horses and lake and —" Their voices trailed off as the three ran across the field.

"How different parents are," Kelly commented to Kirk that evening. "I dread seeing some of them come. I almost wish there wasn't a visiting day! Yet for the parents who really care, and for their kids, it makes all the difference."

"It's hard on the ones who don't have parents."

They all knew he was referring to David. The staff had met for a few moments following dinner to discuss any problems.

"Don't pity David. I'm taking good care of him." Lydia was quick to resent anything she could take as the slightest slur.

"Yes you are, Lydia. So is Tom." Kirk looked at the tall man with appreciation. "All of you are doing a great job. I only wish there was more of a follow-up from here. Some of these kids go back into pretty bad situations. They can gain strength and self-confidence at Alpine Meadows, but will it hold over in their daily lives?"

Tom had been silent until now. "If I could do anything I wanted to do with my life, it would be to have a place like this, not just for a summer, but for always. I'd get every lonely or mistreated or hurt kid in the world and see they had a fighting chance." His impassioned voice stirred them all.

"And I'd be right there, helping." Lydia looked around the circle of faces and her own face hardened. "I know you don't believe me, but it's true." With a flash of green sandals she was gone, banging the door behind her.

The rest of the staff refused to look at Tom, but he said quietly, "She means it, you know. Alpine Meadows heals in more than one way."

He stepped through the door, letting in an evening ray of stray sunlight. Through the screen they could see him overtake Lydia, stop her, then walk toward their dorm, his arm around her shoulders.

Kelly found her eyes were wet. "Tom's right. There's all kinds of healing taking place at Alpine Meadows." She looked up to catch Kirk watching her in an odd manner, his expression unreadable.

When the other staff members had gone, he detained her.

"Is Alpine Meadows doing what it should for you, Kelly?"

She made no pretense of misunderstanding. "I think so."

To her disappointment, he merely said, "Good. Now, about this campout we're finally having after so many postponements. What's the best way to handle it? I know you'd like to go, but we need someone here with those who aren't ready. We still have half a dozen who can't make it overnight, even being trucked in. I know Lydia hates that sort of thing, so we'll leave her here. The Cunninghams will stay, too. Would you stay this time, Kelly? Next time we'll trade off and keep Marilou here."

"I'll stay. I don't know how things will work out with Lydia, but I'll really try. If we're the only two counselors, we'll just have to work together."

"I'm sure you can handle it." Kirk didn't even seem to be listening. "You know, this campout is the real test. The ones who have recuperated the most have hiked and swum and learned camp chores. If they can make it on an overnighter, we can dismiss a whole batch of them. The weather's supposed to be good for Tuesday and Wednesday. We'll get ready tomorrow and leave early Tuesday morning. Bob and I'll ride with those who can handle horses. Tom can help Marilou with the others and drive the truck."

Kelly thought fast. "Is David going?"

Kirk shook his head regretfully. "Not this time. He just isn't ready. He asked me if he could go and I had to tell him no. It was the hardest thing I'd ever done. Kelly, I really thought he was improving. I still think he is, mentally. Lydia and Tom have been a tremendous help. He clings to them. But somehow that leg situation isn't getting along the way I'd hoped."

"I know." Kelly's shoulders slumped. "Next time we're in Seattle I want him checked again. In spite of the rubs and exercise, even the swimming, it's slow, too slow. I had been ready to recommend brace removal, but I just can't, not yet. I don't know why the healing slowed down. He's certainly been faithful about doing what he's told."

"I just wish he could go. Well, I'd better

get something done." But his eyes were still troubled as he went out, leaving Kelly feeling defeated.

Suddenly she was homesick. Frighteningly, violently homesick. If only Dad were here! He could tell why David was progressing as slowly as he was. Oh, the Seattle surgeons were tops. And the Alpine physician was excellent. But if only Dad were here!

Kelly wished for Dr. Lawrence even more after the visit to Seattle. The surgeon and a special team examined David. When they came out, Kelly caught their dismay.

"He's going to have to have another operation in time," the surgeon said. "Right now we can only wait for him to be strong enough."

"Oh, no! He's been through so much!"

"I know." The surgeon looked straight at Kelly. "Are you by any chance familiar with the work of Dr. Lawrence of San Antonio? He's been doing wonders in the field of bone surgery and follow-up for children. I wish he could see David."

Kelly's eyes shone. "He's my father."

"Is there any chance of getting him out here? I know we can handle David's case, but there's this new thing Dr. Lawrence has been working with I'd like to see used. You're probably familiar with it."

"Not fully. I know he's been working a great deal on some new techniques. But I've been gone since spring."

"Why don't you call and ask him to come if he can get away? If he can't, ask him to send someone to work with our own team." The surgeon hesitated. "In the meantime, keep David in braces. He's to continue his exercises, be outdoors, but no rough stuff."

Kirk could see Kelly's disappointment. She was quiet on the way home. It wasn't until after David had fallen asleep, much as he had done that day so long ago, that she spoke about him.

"He's going to be terribly let down. We had promised he could go on the next campout. It's this week, isn't it?"

"Yes. The last one went off so well, we dismissed a batch of campers. By the way, we'll be getting new ones more in a dribble from now on than as batches."

"I hate to tell David."

It was even harder than they had thought. His sturdy feet in their braces were planted apart, his arms folded. "You said I could go next time. This is next time. You pwomised!" A missing tooth gave him a temporary lisp.

"I know, David, but the surgeon says you're going to need some more work."

Fear sprang into the blue eyes. "Then I'll never get to go! I'll be back there and hurt and never get to go, not forever!"

Kirk could feel himself losing control. The little boy's blue eyes and blond hair gleamed in the sun. He looked so determined, so scared.

Kelly fought back her tears. She couldn't cry in front of David. "Sometimes we can't do what we want, David. This is one of those times. We want you to get strong and well."

"I am stwong and well. See!" He ran across the field and back.

"Yes, but we want those braces off." Kelly knew he wasn't being convinced. "David, do you know that this time the only ones left here in camp will be Lydia and the Cunninghams and you and me? Most of our campers have gone home and we won't get any more for a few days. Think of all the fun we'll have, just the five of us."

David scuffed his foot on the ground. "I want to go on the campout with the others." He turned and walked away, his head down, dejection in every movement.

"If I live to be a hundred, I'll never get used to seeing kids disappointed." Kirk's voice was disturbingly near.

"Me, neither. But there's no other choice.

107

Sometimes a person has to do what's best, even if they don't like it."

"Speaking from personal experience?"

She stopped short at his question, but not before he held up a hand.

"Sorry I asked that, Kelly. You're doing fine."

That's what he thinks. But Kelly didn't say the words aloud.

The next day dawned beautiful. Before eight o'clock everyone had eaten and the overnight campers started off. Lydia stood with her arm around David, waving at the horseback riders and truckers.

Kelly saw David's chin start to quiver, his eyes fill with tears. He broke away from Lydia and dashed around the corner of the big log house.

Lydia started for him, but was stopped by Gramps's comment, "Let him go, Lydia. Granny'll give him a cooky or something and he'll feel better."

For the first time Kelly and Lydia were in full sympathy. The look they shared was one of concern for a small disappointed boy who would be the only child left in camp while everyone else went off for a good time.

Kirk had asked Kelly if she wanted to go, but she refused. If David couldn't go, she should be in camp. Now she watched the group disappear through the trees and down the dusty road, wondering what special activity they could cook up for David.

Chapter 7

The hammock swayed violently, threatening to upset Kelly. She opened her eyes to the late afternoon's slanting rays, forcing her heavy lids to stay open. Good heavens, had she slept all morning and afternoon since the group left for the campout?

It had been so quiet, the hammock so inviting, she hadn't been able to resist dropping down. She hadn't meant to stay there all day! It would have been a good time for doing laundry and taking care of some other personal items. But her eyes closed again.

"Kelly, wake up!" The urgency of the voice, the shaking of the hammock, opened her eyes wide.

"Lydia, what's wrong?" Part of Kelly's mind registered that Lydia looked far different from the young woman who had first come to Alpine Meadows. She had long since packed away her glamorous playclothes for blue jeans and T-shirts and such. But never had her blonde hair hung in strings the way it did now.

"Have you seen David?" The usually petulant mouth trembled.

"David? No. He ran to Granny Cunningham when we told the others good-bye. Wasn't he at lunch?"

Lydia's pale face got even whiter. "No. I fell asleep in the cabin. Must have been exhausted." She managed a wan smile. "I love this work, but it is exhausting."

Kelly could agree with that, considering how she had slept. "But what about David?"

"About an hour ago I woke and went to the kitchen. Granny and Gramps were surprised when I asked about lunch — and David. I thought maybe I'd get a snack to hold me until dinner. Granny said David came in at lunchtime or a little before and told her he was taking me on a picnic, and could we have an outdoor lunch? She packed a huge lunch in a basket. She said she watched him start toward our cabin, but the phone rang. That's the last she saw of him."

Two big tears rolled down Lydia's face. "Oh, Kelly, where is he?"

Kelly thought fast. "He wanted to go on the campout more than anything. You don't suppose —" Her mouth dried up at the idea.

In moments they were racing across the field, into the Jacksons' cabin with its woodsy smell. "Which is his room?"

"Right in here." Lydia stepped in, closely followed by Kelly.

"What's missing?" Kelly looked around the shipshape little cubicle with three beds, not knowing where to start.

"Everything seems here. Blanket from his bed, jacket." Lydia was rummaging through the clothing hung on hooks at the end of the bed. "Even the hunting knife Tom gave him. He never leaves that."

"I'm afraid he might have tried to follow the others."

It didn't seem possible a human face could hold so much agony. Kelly felt her first true rush of compassion for this woman, over-riding all the dislike of the past. "Don't worry, Lydia. We'll find him. The first thing to do is talk with the Cunninghams."

"I have." Lydia dropped to the neatly made cot. "Why did I ever drop down for a nap? I thought David was with Granny. He loves her. I didn't dream I'd sleep more than a few minutes! It's all my fault, Kelly!" She buried her face in her hands.

Kelly forced steel into her voice. "Sitting there blaming yourself isn't going to find David. Get some hiking shoes on. We'll ask Gramps to go one way, we'll take the other. Gramps can take your car and follow the way the truck went. I don't think David would try following the horses. He would know he couldn't make it."

Lydia sprang up, hope in her eyes. "Even with several hours' start, Gramps will overtake him on the road. He can't walk very fast and he'll have to stop and rest a lot. You're right. We should have him home before dark." She valiantly controlled a sob. "If I ever get my hands on that kid, I'll never let him out of my sight again! You can't know what he means to me."

Kelly's answer was quiet. "I think I do, Lydia." But there was no time for discussion. Already the late sun was casting rosy banners in the sky, heralding night shadows.

Gramps was firm. "You girls follow the horse trail. Take your time. Mark a tree if you have to leave the trail or anything."

His eyes were serious. "There are some angry clouds coming up in the west. We may get a storm. The last thing we need is for you two to get lost. I'll probably find David, but you get back here before dark. Take slickers and heavy flashlights in case the storm comes. If it does, don't stand under a tall tree, they're lightning bait."

He looked at them dubiously. "I shouldn't even let you go, but you won't have any trouble if you stay on the trail."

"We will," Kelly promised. "I know I'm still a tenderfoot and Lydia isn't much better."

She was rewarded with a weak smile from Lydia.

"You needn't be so polite, Kelly. I don't know anything about the woods, except that they're big and scary and full of wild animals." She stopped short, her color fading. "Come on, let's go." Without a backward glance she headed for her cabin to pick up her slicker and flashlight.

"Good stuff in her," Gramps said to Kelly. "Wouldn't be surprised if she turned out all right after all."

Gramp's words rang in Kelly's ears a short while later, as she followed Lydia down the trail. Did it take danger to a loved one to turn people into what they ought to be? She shuddered. David, small, still a little frail in spite of his improvement. What if he had not taken the road? Could they find him, especially if a storm hit?

Never had Kelly seen a sky darken as rapidly as it did that evening. One minute there was light coming through the trees; the next, there was a mighty roar and clouds all around them.

"Shall we go back?"

The wind whipped Kelly's words, but

Lydia managed to understand. "I can't. If David's out here . . ." The rest of her sentence was snatched away by the elements.

Fortunately the horse trail was rather wide and packed down. The walking wasn't difficult until it began to rain. Then needles underfoot suddenly became slippery, treacherous, even though they were wearing their rubber-soled hiking shoes.

Finally Lydia stopped. "Kelly, we'll have to rest."

"There's a sheltered area just ahead," Kelly shouted, flashing her light. "I think it's just around this bend, a little cave. Kirk showed it to me."

"But what about David?"

"We can't see to find him, Lydia. He's a smart little boy. He'll take cover somewhere. And, as you said, we need to rest." She held out her hand. "Here, let me go first. My flashlight's strongest."

Wrists gripped, they turned the bend. "It's just across this slide area," Kelly said. "We'll cross and get in the cave until the rain stops. If the moon comes out, we can see enough to follow the trail."

Lydia hesitated. "Isn't it supposed to be dangerous to cross a slide area when it's wet?"

"We don't have a choice. Besides, it's only about ten feet." Kelly stepped forward. A few loose pebbles rattled beneath her feet. "It's okay, Lydia. Hang on to me."

The next moment a giant crash sounded through the forest. A slow rumble filled the air, a gathering of momentum of all nature's forces for an onslaught of the earth. Kelly could feel the trail slipping beneath her.

She regained her footing. "Run, Lydia, run!"

It was too late. The moving earth was too fast. With a roar and slide, the whole trail section gave way, throwing both girls down the hill. Kelly managed to hang on to Lydia. They must not be separated, not now. If they were — she refused to complete the thought.

A rock bit into Kelly's arm. Another bounced off one ankle, causing an involuntary cry of pain. There was a sudden stop — then merciful oblivion.

When Kelly opened her eyes again, she thought she had gone blind. It was pitch black, the velvety softness that oppresses.

"Lydia!"

There was no answer.

She frantically clawed as far around her as she could reach. There was no sign of the other girl.

"Lydia, Lydia!"

From a nearby mountain came the faint reply, "Lydia, Lydia!"

Then all was silent. Kelly tried to think. When had she released Lydia's hand? Where was she? Why had she stopped? She didn't dare move. It felt as if she were impaled on a tree branch. What if it gave way, throwing her even farther down the mountain?

With uncertain fingers, Kelly groped at the area around her again. This time she came in contact with cold, hard metal — a flashlight! She pressed the button. Nothing.

"Please, God!" She tried again and was rewarded with a flickering light, just enough to see a few feet away from her.

A dull moan reached her and she whipped around. Lydia lay just beyond touch, bent at a grotesque angle. Was she seriously hurt?

Every instinct in Kelly rose, every nursing skill and oath she had ever taken. She must get to Lydia. Cautiously she shone the flashlight around. She had been right. A big log had wedged itself in the middle of the slide.

Both of them were caught on the upper side. Even as Kelly moved, the log moved a bit, filling her with fear. She had to get to the other side of the slide — the side near Lydia — and bring Lydia with her!

Inch by inch, dragging an ankle that felt

like lead, Kelly made her way to Lydia. Steeling herself against stopping to see how badly hurt Lydia was, she gained the safety of the woods beside the slide area. Good! She could just reach Lydia's shoulders.

It was the hardest work she had ever done. Unnerved by the storm, weakened by her own injuries, Kelly forced herself to pull Lydia to safe ground. She tasted the sickish taste of blood and knew her lips were cut. She had bitten them herself without having been conscious of what she was doing.

"We made it!" Kelly's exultant shout was hardly above a whisper.

Before the words left her throat, there was the dreaded sound of loose gravel. She shone the flashlight back. The log that had held them was slowly sliding, then gaining momentum. In the space of a heartbeat Kelly saw their perch go crashing down the mountainside. There was a moment of stillness, then BOOM! The log must have dropped a long distance to land, broken and destroyed.

Kelly sank back against Lydia. "Thank God!" What if they had been on that log? What if . . .

Stop it, Kelly Lawrence! You have to go ahead! You aren't out of danger yet! She grasped Lydia with superhuman strength and pulled her back from the edge of the slide, working her way until they were firmly resting against a huge tree. If it were the tallest one in the forest, they would still have to stay under it, Kelly thought. She couldn't move one inch more.

With the light of the weakened flashlight, Kelly examined Lydia as best she could. Outside of a huge discolored bruise on her forehead, she appeared to be all right. Evidently something had banged her on their wild ride down the slide.

Kelly stifled a nervous giggle at the thought of how they must have looked, being tossed about until the welcoming log had caught them. It was no time for such childish games, imagining such situations. They had to get out of this mess.

"Wh-where are we?" Lydia had regained consciousness and seen Kelly's face above her in the dim light.

"Somewhere on the side of a mountain, or I suppose it might be a hill out here."

"The trail —" With an effort Lydia shook her head. "Ooh! It hurts!"

"You got banged up pretty good."

"How about you?"

"I'm okay," Kelly told her. "One ankle got hit by something. And maybe bits of stone or branch gouged into it." She didn't add she shuddered to think of what was also in that cut ankle. Without water to bathe it in, infection could be a real problem.

"What now?" Lydia asked.

"We stay here until morning. Then —" For the first time Kelly's courage slipped, but she recovered immediately. "Then we see."

It was the longest, strangest night of their lives. The storm subsided, then stopped. Every tree and bush was dripping wet. Inside their slickers, the girls were miserable. Kelly's ankle hurt. Lydia's head throbbed.

As the first sign of dawn appeared, Lydia roused from the stupor she had sunk into a little while earlier.

"Kelly, I don't know what's going to happen. They won't even be looking for us here. They would think the slide came before or after we crossed. Whatever does happen, I want you to know I appreciate what you did. You could have let me go and maybe not been hurt. It's what I deserved from you."

"Don't be ridiculous!" Kelly's voice was sharp to hide the tears behind it. "We're in this together."

Lydia didn't seem to have heard her. "I was jealous, you know. Kirk, Bob, Marilou, the Cunninghams, even Tom thought you were swell. I wanted them to love me the way they did you." She was frankly crying.

"You were right about what you said to Marilou. When I found out I couldn't have kids, part of me died. Tom wanted a lot of them. I did, too. It was all I had to give him — and then it wasn't to be."

"All you had to give him!" Kelly was incredulous. "Lydia, you're beautiful! You have everything going for you."

"So what? I've seen it isn't beauty that holds husbands. It's wives who have kids, who are real mothers and homemakers."

"So you tried to show him how attractive you were by letting him see how much other men liked you."

"Yes." In the pale morning light, her head came up. "But no more. When I get back to Alpine Meadows, Tom Jackson is going to know how much I love him. I made fun of Marilou for hugging Bob all the time. Wait till you see what I'm going to do!"

Kelly couldn't help but laugh outright. Lydia looked sheepish, then joined her.

"Kelly, if it weren't for the fact that we're hurt and stranded, I'd be *glad* all this happened." She clapped her hand to her mouth. "What am I saying? I meant, because it had made me think. But David! What about David?"

"I don't know, Lydia. I just don't know." Soberly Kelly faced facts. "Hopefully he is with the Cunninghams. If he spent the night out, with his own problems . . ." She could see Lydia's convulsive swallow, the way she licked her lips. "We have to get out of here ourselves and maybe find him. But how?"

Lydia got to her feet, throwing off hesitance and fear. "Kelly, can you walk?"

"I don't know." Kelly got up, put her weight on her ankle, and moaned as it sent thrusts of pain into her leg.

"Here, let me look at that."

Kelly sat down. Then Lydia examined her leg and gasped. The first ray of sun across the little glade was no redder or angrier than the streaks starting up Kelly's leg.

"Blood poisoning! Kelly, where's that first aid kit you had?"

"Merrily falling down the mountainside, I suppose." She deliberately kept her tone light. "The streaks aren't too far up yet. But we have to get out of here."

Kelly would never forget Lydia's look and promise. "We will, Kelly. I'll get you out of this. It was my fault David left and that you're even out of camp, hurt in the woods. I'll get you out of this if my life depends on it." She grimaced. "Trite phrase. But I really mean it."

"I know you do, Lydia." Suddenly Kelly was willing to let Lydia take charge. She could feel some fever starting. Her throat was hot and dry. "I wonder if there's any water anywhere around?"

"There should be." Lydia looked at the slope before them. "All those creeks that run into the lake — one of them should come from up here. I'll go see."

The next moment Lydia was slipping and sliding down the needled slope. After an eternity she crawled back, panting but triumphant. "There's water down there, all right. But I'll have to get you to it." She stared at Kelly appraisingly. "Did you ever go tobogganing?"

"Tobogganing!"

"No, I haven't lost my senses, Kelly. I just have to get you down to that water." Lydia was jerking off her slicker. "Now lean on me and sit on this." She got her slicker under Kelly. "Cross your feet and keep up that bad ankle!"

Their descent was simpler than it had sounded. Lydia went ahead, pulling Kelly on the slicker by one of the sleeves. Even so, Kelly was exhausted when they reached the ledge below overlooking the stream.

"It's not a creek, it's a river!" Kelly exclaimed.

"That's right." Lydia was busy working their way the last few feet down. "These mountain creeks grow into rivers pretty rapidly when it rains like it did last night."

"What on earth are you doing?" Kelly asked a little later, staring at the curious contraption in Lydia's hands.

"Making you a water bag." She held up her trophy. "See?"

It was ingenious. She had managed to rip out a slicker sleeve and by folding it and using a safety pin from her jeans had made a waterproof bag. Seconds later it was filled. Kelly's hands and face were bathed, and she was sipping ice cold water. It seemed to restore her senses.

Lydia had gone for more water and bathed the ankle. "If only I knew something about herbal medicine," she sighed. "I know there are leaves and stuff to stop poison, but I don't know which ones." She looked helplessly around her.

"I don't either. We'll just have to hope your washing it out will help." But there wasn't much conviction in Kelly's voice. In spite of the water, she knew an infection was raising her temperature higher all the time.

"Okay, boss, what now?" Kelly looked up at Lydia, trying to grin. "I never expected to be leaning on you."

"Maybe that's the trouble. No one ever has." Lydia abandoned her self-inspection.

Looking toward the cliff they had come down, she shook her head. "No help up there." She took matches from her pocket. They were sodden, useless. "None there either."

Suddenly she whirled toward the stream that had grown to river proportions. In the same motion she began stripping off her jeans.

"No, Lydia, you can't!" Kelly had divined her intention.

"There's no choice." Lydia threw her jeans to one side. "Glad I put on my bathing suit under my jeans yesterday — I thought I'd go for a swim. And I wouldn't want to shock Granny by appearing in the clearing in just my unmentionables!"

Kelly choked back a cry of admiration for the slim, tanned woman, now clad in her swimsuit. "You can't go, Lydia! It could mean your life."

"And if I don't go, it means yours. We don't have a way to signal. No one will look for us here. The way I figure, this is the creek that runs into the lake from the falls. I can't go downstream any further. I might get caught in the whirlpool above the falls. I have to cross here. I'll start just above the bend, make for the big rock in the middle, then let the current take me around the bend and to the other side."

"And if it doesn't?"

"I will at least have tried." She smiled at Kelly, confidence in her look. "It's the one thing I do well. I've always been a strong swimmer. *Kelly, I'm going to make it!*"

Before Kelly could protest again, Lydia had raced for the river, dashed inside, and headed for the big rock in the middle. She made it, paused to rest, waved her hand, and plunged back into the water. The last Kelly saw of her was one tanned arm stroking hard as the current caught her and swept her around the bend.

Chapter 8

As Kirk waved good-bye to the little group staying in Alpine Meadows the day of the campout, Kelly's face gleamed in the sunlight. She was even more beautiful than when she had come. The hollows in her cheeks had filled out; the dark shadows under her eyes were gone. She was tanned and rested.

I wonder if she would be happy here for the rest of her life, he thought. Kirk smiled grimly to himself. Kelly didn't even like him most of the time, and here he was planning their future together! When had he first known she was the woman he wanted?

The feelings he'd once had for Lydia were washed-out moonlight compared to the full force of sunlit love he felt for Kelly. She was everything in the world to him — and she might still be in love with that San Antonio doctor.

Only time would prove whether she could get over whatever had sent her running to Alpine Meadows. She was not the loving-and-leaving kind. If she had promised to marry Dr. Harrington, it was because he was everything she wanted. Something tragic must have happened.

Lydia had mentioned the giving of a wrong medication. Kirk couldn't imagine Kelly being so careless. It wasn't in her. She was the kind to make sure the care she gave her patients was tops.

Fortunately the campers who rode horseback were competent. So was Bob Campbell, who rode by, grinning. "This is the life, Kirk!" He waved his sombrero. "Me for the high country!"

Kirk laughed. Bob and Marilou Campbell were invaluable. So was Tom Jackson. Lydia — he frowned. She did an outstanding job with "her boys." If only she could relax, unbend, quit trying to prove herself to the adults! Maybe being in camp for two days with David, the Cunninghams, and Kelly would help. No men around to impress.

"Hey, Kirk!" A freckled-faced, tow-headed boy waited at the next turn. "We're almost there, right?"

"How'd you know, Steve?"

"Wally told me from last time when I couldn't make it. But I'm making it now, ain't I?"

"Aren't," Kirk corrected automatically but with a grin. "You sure are making it. You'll be going home next week."

"Yeah." A big smile spread over Steve's face. "Don't get me wrong, I really like it up here. But I sure miss Mom and Pops and the kids. I'll be glad to get home."

"That's fine, Steve. You should feel that way. Just don't forget your friends here."

The freckled face turned solemn. "I won't. I wish you had camp for well kids, maybe on weekends during the winter or something. Then we could all come back."

Kirk felt as if a lightning bolt had struck him. "Steve, that's a great idea." His mind raced ahead. "We could keep the road plowed when we got snow. There's bus service to Alpine and we'd pick up campers there in the wagon."

"Or with a jeep and bobsled if you had to!" Steve's eyes caught fire. "Kirk, you have plenty of close hills to make into easy ski runs and sledding hills. And the lake freezes over for skating, doesn't it?"

"Yes. Yes, it does. I remember skating on it a long time ago, after I had come back from the hospital."

"Then it's all settled. Okay? Do I get to be your first winter weekend guest?" The big smile faded. "Hey, I couldn't come without my family wanting to come, too. What about a family camp?"

"Family camp?"

"Sure. Instead of a bunch of kids, use the dorms for families during the winter. Build on some more space and you could handle at least four big families, or groups, every weekend. People would get reservations ahead. I bet you'd be booked all winter. Lots of folks can't afford the prices at a big lodge with all the fancy equipment. If you could keep prices down . . . but then I guess you wouldn't make much money that way." His face fell.

Kirk's brain was doing circles. "If I could break even and keep expenses paid for in the winter months, it would be enough for a while. In the future I could add more cabins. Steve, old buddy, you may just have started the Alpine Meadows Winter Sports Camp for families."

"I sure hope so!" Steve dug his heels in his horse's flanks. "Giddap." He turned in the saddle. "I have to tell Bob. I bet he and his wife would stay!"

Kirk rode the rest of the way to the campsite only vaguely aware of the summer beauty around him. Even the wild roses he loved couldn't lure him from his thoughts.

What if he did as Steve had laughingly suggested? Would Bob and Marilou stay? They wouldn't be needed as counselors. How could they be used? What about Tom and Lydia? The Cunninghams, of course, were part of Alpine Meadows.

Kirk's heart lurched. What about Kelly? He would definitely want a nurse, especially that nurse. Would she stay? Her agreement was for the summer. Would she be able to stand the cold winters so close to Mt. Rainier?

"She'll stay," he told an inquisitive chipmunk. "I'm going to marry her." His decision was in the air, spoken aloud. Now all he had to do was carry it out. He laughed at his own brashness.

There was a long way between now and winter. He'd keep Kelly as long as he could professionally, but in the meantime, he would also show her what a magnificent place Alpine Meadows could be.

She already loved it, he knew that. His blood raced at the thought of her running through the snow, tumbling into his arms after a snowball fight, curled up on the hearth of the big log house. Why not? If a person worked hard enough at anything, there was no reason he couldn't achieve it.

A little smile started. He would marry Kelly Lee Lawrence, spend the rest of his life here helping kids, and someday have some of his own. She might as well get used to the idea.

"Hey, Kirk, what's the big idea?" In his daydream he had ridden right past Bob and the others!

"A lot on my mind." He winked warningly at Steve, giving him a high sign not to discuss the winter sports camp.

Steve nodded, his face settling into lines of responsibility from having a secret. Kirk noticed how the boy whistled as camp chores began.

The truckers had already arrived and started setting up camp. Marilou had hobo stew started. Biscuits in a dutch oven were baking over the coals, filling the air with their aroma. Marilou was an organizer. Every camper was busy with an assigned task. Not a word of grumbling was heard.

How different from some groups! This group accepted each other's limitations, making up for them with extra help where needed. Although, Kirk had to admit, right now there weren't many limitations. This group of guests was ready to be dismissed.

He spoke of it to them later. "You know, you're all ready to graduate."

The different reactions interested him. Some looked eager, as Steve had done. Others were apprehensive. One of the girls slid closer to Marilou.

"Are we really ready to graduate, Kirk?"

Steve wore that same air of maturity he had gained in the past few weeks.

"Kelly says you are. Everyone in camp except David is ready to go home."

"David doesn't have a home anyway, does he, Kirk?"

"Yes, he does." Tom's voice broke the silence before Kirk could answer. "My wife and I are going to adopt David if the authorities will let us."

"Hey, great! He's a neat little kid."

Smiles and nods showed approval.

But Steve wasn't through with his questions. "Kirk, how'd you happen to start this camp for cr— for kids you knew needed a little extra boost?"

Kirk's face was in shadow.

Later Marilou would tell Kelly, "I had to fight back tears. He was so obviously reliving what he had gone through as a child."

Now Kirk spoke softly. "Steve, when I was a kid I had a problem. A lot of people, including doctors, said I'd never walk again. I didn't buy it. I told them I was going to walk and swim and ride and do everything just the way we've done it today."

His voice took on an unconscious longing. "There was one doctor, a great man even then, more important now. He believed me and in me. He spent hours helping me, giving

133

me self-confidence, trying over and over."

Beads of sweat from the memory of his hard efforts stood out on Kirk's face. "Together we did it. I made up my mind if I could ever help others the way he helped me, I'd do it. When my grandparents died and left me Alpine Meadows, I wrote to Dr. Lawrence and —"

"Dr. Lawrence! Is Kelly Lawrence any relation?"

"She is his daughter."

"So that's why she's so swell. Wow, Kirk, you sure were lucky to have her dad and now have her around!"

Bob, Tom, and Marilou exchanged glances across the campfire at Kirk's answer. "Very lucky, Steve."

In the distance an owl hooted; then the sound of a running motor broke up the mood.

"Hey, Mr. Cunningham, Gramps, what are you doing here?"

There was no answering smile from Gramps. "Kirk, is David here?"

"David!"

The entire camp stared blankly at Mr. Cunningham, worry lines turning down the corners of his mouth.

"Of course not. We left him in camp."

"He didn't stay there. We thought he

might have tried to come up here. Lydia thought he was with Granny. He asked for a big picnic lunch for himself and Lydia and disappeared. He's been gone from camp since just before noon."

He cocked his head to the rising wind. "Bad storm coming up. Lydia and Kelly are out looking for him, following the horse trail. Hated to let them go, but there was no other way." A jagged flash of lightning followed by a crack of thunder drowned out his voice.

"In the tents, kids!" Kirk shouted.

Before the first huge raindrop spattered into the fire, sizzling its way into obscurity, the campers were in the big tents.

"Remember, don't touch the sides and they won't soak through. Everyone in?"

"Yeah!" Steve said. "What about David?"

Kirk had been thinking with the speed of the lightning now playing tag across their campsite.

"Bob and Marilou, you stay with the campers. Tom, you go back with Gramps and watch both sides of the road just in case David's out in this."

"What about the horses?" someone asked.

"We'll turn them loose. They'll go back home on their own. I'm taking my own horse and going back down the trail. How long have the girls been out?"

"Since suppertime," Gramps said. "Had a flat on the way up and had to change it."

"Then they could be at least halfway here." Kirk cast a calculating look at the sky, now opening its faucets into a wild and steady stream. "I'll find them."

Tom was beside him. "Let me go with you, Kirk. It's my wife who's out there."

Kirk hesitated. Tom wasn't too much of a rider, yet he was deeply concerned about Lydia. "Come on. We don't have time to waste."

Their horses hated the trip along the slippery trail in the dark. Even the flashlights Kirk and Tom carried weren't reassuring enough for the horses to easily accept their urging.

They snorted, threw up their heads.

"Hold in your horse, Tom!" Kirk warned, but Tom's determination made up for his lack of skill.

Lydia was out there. He had to find her.

Kirk's heart went out to Tom. If he was concerned about Kelly, what must Tom feel about Lydia? And with David missing on top of it all! Would they never get down this terrible trail that had been so pleasant a few hours earlier?

"They're probably in the cave," he shouted to Tom. "They would have crossed the slide and be on this side of it. Kelly knows about the cave."

Tom just smiled, forcing himself to meet Kirk's attempt at cheer. But that smile was more devastating than he knew. It mirrored Kirk's own feelings — what if they weren't in the cave? What then?

It seemed hours before they reached the cave. There were downed branches on the trail. Kirk and Tom had to lead the horses through. Their task was hindered by the steady beat of rain, the diminishing but still deafening peals of thunder. At last they reached it.

"Here," Kirk shouted.

They stepped inside, shone their flashlights around. Nothing. It was empty, bare, dry, seemingly untouched by the wild storm.

Kirk had never admired a person more than he did Tom at that moment. In the dim light his face looked ghastly, but no sign came from his lips, only a, "What do we do now?"

"We wait until morning. It's suicide to cross that slide area ahead in this kind of weather. I'll show you."

They stepped back outside, tied up the horses, and walked around the next bend to the slide area.

Kirk flashed his light, then froze in place. For a moment his heart stopped. *The trail across the slide was gone, buried under a piece of mountain that had slid down from above!*

Tom's control broke for the first time. "They aren't under that!"

"Don't be a fool!" Kirk lashed out, fear for Kelly and Lydia spreading through him. "The chances are they got this far, saw this, and turned back."

"I hope so."

Kirk forced iron control over himself. "We'll wait in the cave until daylight. It won't be long now. The storm's passing. Then we'll plan what to do. We might be able to lead the horses across this. I don't know. There's nothing else we can do now."

Every second ticking away on the two men's watches brought fresh agony. There was nothing to say, so they didn't talk. Each was busy with personal feelings, the struggle to push back total despair.

Uppermost in their minds, in spite of Kirk's assurance, was the gruesome thought: What if the girls had been in the slide? They had had plenty of time to get across it. If they hadn't, they would have returned to camp. Suppose they had come across? Why hadn't they stopped in the cave?

"If something happens to her, it will mean

the end of everything for me." Tom's voice was not bitter, just stating a fact.

"And for me," Kirk said, acknowledging his love for Kelly. "Kelly Lawrence is everything I hoped for and dreamed of. Maybe that's why I won't accept they aren't all right. If I'm wrong —"

A strong hand gripped his in the darkness.

"Kirk, when we're out of here, I won't be able to say this. You know I can't put my words together and show feelings much. But the finest thing you ever did was step out of the picture when Lydia turned to me. I know you could have held her at the time, if you had really wanted to."

"You're wrong, Tom. For what it's worth, even though Lydia threw me over with the excuse she wanted more prestige and all that, I guess I always knew it was you she really loved. I hoped being up here would help."

"It has. Through David and the others, we've started becoming a family. Now — well, I guess we'll just have to wait."

Never had a morning been more welcomed, a sun more rejoiced over.

"Thank God for that!" Kirk's exclamation roused Tom, who had been so lost in thought he didn't realize the night and storm were over.

Yet the same sun that warmed the land brought to their sight the utter destruction of the trail section. Great trees had been uprooted and hurled downward, leaving in their wake a treacherous, steep piece of ground.

"We can't cross that. We'll have to go on the assumption they came across and got off the trail, or else they went back home."

Kirk took the binoculars he always carried from his saddlebag. Slowly, carefully, he scanned every inch of the mountainside from where they stood. Tom walked back and forth in the immediate area, looking for something, anything, that would betray the girls' presence.

"What did you find?" Kirk asked, seeing him holding something in his hand.

"Nothing, I guess." Tom started to toss it away, then peered at it again. "Is that a bloodstain on this rag?"

Kirk's heart leaped, but no faster than his arm flew out to Tom. "Where did you find this?"

"Down there." Tom pointed down several feet. "I thought maybe someone threw away some litter."

"No one has used the trail except us — and our campers don't litter."

Now Kirk was on the alert. Getting down

on his hands and knees, he examined every inch of ground. "Tom, something slid down this mountainside, and look! Footprints!" In the soft earth ahead were prints going down.

"Don't bring the horses! Leave them here!" Kirk said.

Tom needed no warning. He had learned during the night that Kirk Long knew what he was talking about. Now he willingly followed instructions.

"Easy, dig in your heels, Tom. This is still slippery, with the needles and mud."

One step. Another. Another. The way down seemed endless. They were panting when they stepped out on the little ledge above the swollen creek that had become a river.

"Look!" Tom's fingers dug into Kirk's arm.

Kirk needed no direction. He ran the remaining few feet down, ignoring the branches in his way.

On the sandy bar, back from the water's edge, a motionless figure lay face down. Nearby a crude water bag formed from a yellow slicker sleeve held a few mouthfuls of water. Tangled dark hair spread over the figure lying in the sun; one scratched hand clutched the water bag.

"Kelly!" Kirk shouted. Was she dead?

The figure stirred. The eyes opened, dark, filled with pain. "Kirk! I thought you'd never come!" she sighed, and the eyelids drooped again.

Kirk gathered her in his arms. "Kelly, my darling! You're safe! You're safe, do you understand?"

There was no response. The relief of his coming had done what nothing else could do. Kelly had relaxed enough to sink into oblivion.

"Look at her leg!" Tom's cry horrified his companion.

With a muttered imprecation, Kirk carried her to the river's edge, bathed her burning face with water.

"Get the first aid kit in my saddlebag!"

Tom was halfway up the slope before Kirk finished speaking. In an incredibly short time he was back, his own burning question withheld. Kirk ripped open the case, found liquid soap and cleansed the wound, shuddering at the red streaks staining Kelly's ankle.

"We've got to get her out of here." He looked up, caught by the position of Tom's body. Tom was staring at something.

"*What is that?*" Kirk asked.

Tom couldn't answer. He could only hold up the discarded pair of women's jeans from the sand, his face working.

"Kelly!" Kirk shook her. "Kelly, you have to tell us. Where is Lydia?"

But the eyelids remained motionless. Kelly Lawrence was past telling anyone anything.

Chapter 9

"Lydia has gone for help the only way she knew." Tom's constricted throat finally let go of the words. He walked to the river's edge, picked up a pair of hiking shoes.

"But why? She must have known there wasn't a chance in a —" Kirk could have strangled himself for saying it.

"That wouldn't stop her." Tom sagged, then straightened. "She was right, Kirk. If Kelly doesn't get attention soon, she's going to die or lose her leg at the very least. Once down here, there's no way Lydia could get Kelly back up."

Kirk's mind was clearing, trying to reconstruct the scene. "They would know we wouldn't be looking for them down here, at least not in time to help Kelly. Tom, how good a swimmer is Lydia? I've seen her at camp, but what about long-distance swimming against odds?"

"The best. She could have been Olympic material if she wanted to do it. She didn't."

"Then she may just make it. See that rock in midstream? She would head for that. On the other side, the current could take her around the bend, and possibly to shore. I don't want to give you too much hope, but Lydia could make it!"

"Thanks, Kirk." Tom swallowed hard. "I just wish I'd told her oftener how much I love her." He turned abruptly from the river. "We have to get Kelly out of this hole."

The two men worked like wheels on a bicycle, in perfect unison. Between them they got Kelly up the slope, back to the slide area.

"We can't take her across there," Kirk said breathing hard. "We'll have to take her back to the campsite and pray they haven't already left for home in the truck!"

Kelly never regained consciousness during the horseback ride that was even more of a nightmare than the storm the night before. Broken phrases came from the parched lips, still feverish in spite of the water Kirk kept pouring over them. "No! No, Lydia — come back!"

A long silence, then: "I can't marry a man I can't respect."

Each word of that sentence struck a blow at Kirk's heart. Then he thought about it. Was she talking about him — or someone else? Kelly was delirious, out of her head. She didn't even know the one who loved her more than life itself rode steadily up over an almost-impossible trail, made even worse by the storm that had raged since Kirk and Tom had crossed it.

Kelly mumbled, "Please, God, send someone."

Kirk's hold tightened, his own heart echoing her prayer, "Please, God, help me get her through."

Tom rode ahead. In spite of his inexperience, he could make better time than the double-burdened horse carrying Kirk and Kelly. He burst back into the campsite as the group was getting the packing finished; the truck was already being warmed up.

"Where's Kirk?" Bob demanded.

"He's bringing Kelly. She's been hurt, caught in a slide." He tried to speak without frightening the campers. "She and Lydia were caught —"

"And Lydia?" There was nothing but concern in Marilou's voice.

"She evidently swam the river to get help. We found her jeans and hiking shoes by the bank. Kelly hasn't been able to tell us anything yet." He turned away, unwilling to meet the pitying gaze of the Campbells.

"Here they are." Tom rushed to the truck, opening a path between campers. Kirk gently laid Kelly on the hastily assembled sleeping bags that would serve as a mattress. "Let's go."

The personnel at the Alpine Hospital weren't prepared for Kirk Long bursting in with Kelly, demanding, "Where's your doctor on duty?"

Most of them had learned to know Kelly as the "Alpine Meadows Nurse," as she had been called jokingly by the waitress long ago. They all knew Kirk. Yet never had they seen the imperturbable man in such a state. With his sleepless eyes, and a day's growth of stubble, he little resembled the usually immaculate man of the forest they knew.

"This doesn't look good," the doctor told Kirk a few minutes later. "How long has it been like this?"

"As near as we can figure, she must have lain out there several hours last night, then all of today." He glanced at a nearby clock. "Good heavens, is it only noon?"

"Yes, but that's bad enough."

"Should we take her into Seattle?" Kirk asked.

The doctor shook his head. "No, we have every facility here to help her, and excellent personnel. Besides, I don't want her moved anymore. She's been through enough."

While he talked, his expert fingers were cleansing, probing. Kelly had been given a

147

local anesthetic. The cut had been deep, filled with dirt.

At last the doctor straightened and gave a medication order. "There. That will start antibiotics into her system. They should begin working right away. She'll be watched closely. If she doesn't respond in a reasonable length of time, then we'll have to operate. It appears I got out everything in the cut, but I also want X-rays to be sure there isn't a chipped or broken bone."

He looked at Kirk keenly. "I suggest you go home. There's nothing you can do here, not now."

Kirk stumbled from the hospital, too weary to even speak. Now that Kelly was out of apparent danger, the whole thing rushed back to him. Lydia, David — they were still missing. What would Tom and Kirk's return home bring?

It was a subdued group that arrived at Alpine Meadows. Between the storm and worry over David, not even the campers had had much sleep. They were glad enough to tumble into bed now. It was left for the adults to discuss what to do.

"If she made it across the river, she just had to walk along until she got here in camp," Gramps reminded them. "She should have been here by now."

The Cunninghams, the Campbells, Tom, and Kirk were gathered outside.

"I'd suggest we split up and work our way along toward the lake," Kirk said. "She would definitely be on this side of it. Probably so exhausted from the swim she couldn't keep going."

"Let's go!" Tom said, but a voice from the doorway stopped him.

"There's no need for that."

"Lydia!"

They all whirled to face her.

Then Tom repeated, "Lydia!" It was barely a whisper.

She looked like a ghost. Her blonde hair hung down in dirty strings. There was a lump on her head the size of a goose egg. Every visible inch of her arms and legs was scratched and filthy.

With a cry Tom was beside her. "Darling, my darling. I thought you were dead!"

Lydia's heart was in her eyes. "I couldn't die, Tom. I had to get help for Kelly — and tell you how much I love you."

Kirk could feel a mist rising, clouding his vision.

But Tom was oblivious to their audience. "Lydia, you're beautiful."

She stared at him, began to laugh, then grew serious.

"But Kelly, you have to help Kelly!"

"Kelly's going to be just fine. Kirk and I found her and she's in the Alpine Hospital."

She sagged against him, then straightened.

"Then I didn't need to swim." She began to laugh again, hysterically. "You would have found us anyway."

"No, Lydia." Kirk responded to the plea in Tom's eyes. "If you hadn't slid Kelly down that bank and taken care of her, I don't know what might have happened." She must not feel her hard struggle had been useless.

With a visible effort she managed to stop laughing. "First I lost David. Then I got Kelly hurt. David. David!" Her eyes widened. "Where is he?"

"We still don't know." Kirk hated the way the color drained from her already too-white face. "But we're going to fan out and find him."

Lydia again leaned on Tom for support. "What a fine mother I turned out to be. Maybe we shouldn't adopt David after all."

"Don't be ridiculous!" The shake Tom gave her was gentle but significant. "Children run away from all kinds of mothers. You're going to be the best in the world!"

"Lydia, why don't you get cleaned up and rest? We'll look for David." Marilou was all compassion, but Lydia shook her head.

"I can't. I lost him, I have to find him." She was obdurate. None of them could talk her out of it.

Marilou said, "At least let me get something from Kelly's nurse's cabin for those scratches and bruises."

Lydia let Marilou lead her away. The eyes of the others followed them as they crossed the field, Lydia gallantly refusing to lean on Marilou, although there was weariness in every step.

Would they ever know what she had gone through in her swim? Kirk wondered. Had there been a moment when she didn't think she could make it? Had she been tempted to give up, to let the current carry her where it would, to stop fighting the rocks and branches that must have been around her?

She couldn't have been so scratched before the swim, not even from the slide. Her jeans would have protected her. Those scratches had come later.

She must have been swept down a lot further than she should have been to take so long getting back to camp. Lydia Jackson was quite a woman. Now if only they could find David!

Afterward no one quite remembered all

the details. They just knew the door of the nurse's cabin flew open and a totally rejuvenated Lydia came flying out, closely followed by Marilou. Across the field the blonde came, like a homing pigeon, straight to Tom — and carrying a small, blue-eyed, golden-haired little boy.

"David!" Tom reached for them both, hugged them hard.

The Cunninghams were openly reaching for them all, thanking God.

It was left for Marilou to explain what happened. "We went in the cabin. He was sitting there. He looked scared and asked, 'Are you awful mad at me?' "

"David, where have you been?" Kirk couldn't bear the suspense any longer. He disengaged David from the Jacksons.

David hung his head, refusing to look at Kirk, scuffing his shoe on the ground. "I — I wanted to be on the campout."

"So?"

"I went up the road. But it was too far. I came back and Granny gave me lunch, for a picnic. But Lydia was asleep. I camped out behind Kelly's cabin. It got dark and rained. I went to my house, but no one was home. So I camped out in my bed in Kelly's cabin."

Granny reached over for the small sinner.

"Why didn't you come in for breakfast, David?"

He looked at her solemnly, one tear ready to spill over. "Everyone went away and left me. I thought you were all mad. So I stayed in the cabin." He looked around the group. "Where's Kelly?"

"She had an accident." Lydia caught Tom's warning look. "She'll be back in a few days. David, don't ever go off again. Okay?"

"Okay." He ran to her, tucking his blond head into the crook of her arm. "Why are you crying? Lydia sad?"

"I'm happy, David. Very happy." With David between them, Tom and Lydia moved off toward their dorm and the rest of their "family."

"I'm going to drive back into Alpine," Kirk said. "When Kelly wakes, she's going to want to know David's safe."

"Better clean up first, buddy." Bob's big grin failed to hide how glad he was everyone had turned up safe. "They might let you in the hospital once looking like you do, but not twice!"

Kirk thought of it as he swung the station wagon into the hospital parking lot forty minutes or so later. He must have looked pretty awful. Yet neither he nor Tom had gone through what Kelly and Lydia had suffered.

Either or both of them could have been killed. Even thinking of it nauseated him. Mountain slides and swollen rivers were part of life at Alpine Meadows. They were to be understood, lived with, and respected. If Kelly ever consented to stay, she had a lot to learn. After this experience, would she view the country he loved as frightening, too dangerous to enjoy?

He had no time for future projections. When he stepped inside, he was greeted by the nurse who had been specialing Kelly when he left.

"How is she?"

"She's going to be fine! Already her fever is showing signs of dropping."

"May I see her?"

"I'm sure it would be all right, except" — she looked a little confused — "the other doctor's with her, of course, and —"

"Other doctor?" Had they called in some- one else?

"Her fiancé." The nurse was all eyes. "We were so surprised! He evidently flew into Seattle at her request, tried to call Alpine Meadows and couldn't reach anyone. He rented a car and drove out. He said it was just a hunch to stop by the hospital and see if she happened to be here. He didn't dream, of course, she would be a patient! He thought she might be helping out or something."

"And his name is —"

"Dr. Harrington. Dr. Brad Harrington. All the way from San Antonio. Isn't it romantic?"

"Very." Kirk forced himself to smile, to coolly say, "Since he's here, I think I won't go in. Keep me posted, will you?"

"Oh, sure. Did you find the little boy?"

"He spent the night in Kelly's cabin."

"Well, if that isn't something," she said. "Kids!"

He walked off, leaving her still mumbling to herself.

He evidently flew into Seattle at her request. The casual words beat over and over in his brain. Kelly had sent for Dr. Harrington. Dr. Brad Harrington, who had been, or was, her fiancé. Kirk's mouth twisted with unbearable pain. Had the absence of a few short weeks made her see how much she cared for the man?

Outside the hospital, Kirk hesitated. He would like to catch a glimpse of the doctor who had come at Kelly's request. He felt like a sneak, leaning back in his car, pretending he was waiting for someone. Sooner or later Dr. Harrington would have to come out! Kirk smiled wryly. When the doctor appeared, he would be waiting.

It still didn't make sense. Kelly ran away from the guy. She said she wasn't going to marry him. In her delirium she had cried out she couldn't marry a man she couldn't respect. Yet here Harrington was, answering Kelly's call. A little smile crossed Kirk's rugged features. With it came an idea. His smile grew broader. Well, why not?

The sun was beginning to set before a likely candidate to be Brad Harrington stepped out of the door. Kirk was out of the car immediately.

"Dr. Harrington?"

The thin, dark-haired man turned, annoyed. "Yes?"

"I'm Kirk Long, Miss Lawrence's employer."

Some of the annoyance faded. "I see." He looked at Kirk. "Was there something you wanted?"

Kirk restrained himself from saying something stupid like "No, just to look you over." Instead he smiled. "I was wondering if you had made arrangements for your stay. We would be happy to have you at Alpine Meadows. Surely, Miss Lawrence has told you a great deal about us."

Not by the movement of a hair did Brad Harrington betray how little he knew of Alpine Meadows, yet Kirk discerned it.

"How good of you." Dr. Harrington cast a contemptuous glance over the contented little town basking in late afternoon sun, surrounded by mountains. "I don't suppose there is much chance of a decent place to stay here in town."

For one moment Kirk considered letting him have it right then and there. "I believe you will be more comfortable at Alpine Meadows."

The doctor unbent a little. "Shall I follow you out? I'll be wanting the car to come in and see Kelly."

"That will be fine." Again Kirk was tempted to give Dr. Harrington the time of his life and take him home over the little-used back road. Once more he overrode his natural feelings in the interest of good manners.

"You have quite a place here," the doctor commented later that evening as he walked with Kirk.

Probably the most exercise he had had in years, Kirk thought. He hated the patronizing remark, the way Dr. Harrington had brushed up his small, silly-looking moustache when he met Marilou and Lydia.

"I intend it to be a lot more. In the meantime, we like it," Kirk said.

"We?"

"My staff and I."

Dr. Harrington looked unutterably bored. "Everyone to his own taste, I'm sure. Nice for a weekend, but I wouldn't want to live here." He abandoned his interest. "Ever spend time in Seattle? Now that's what I call living. Even in my short time there yesterday I could see it had what it takes."

Kirk's voice was as bored as Dr. Harrington's had been. "Oh, yes, I get in a lot. Nice for a weekend, but I wouldn't want to live there."

Dr. Harrington had the grace to color. He changed the subject immediately. "I can't see how Kelly Lawrence could stand it out here as long as she has!"

"Oh?"

If there were danger signals in the comment, Dr. Harrington didn't hear them. "She's a real city girl, always has been, always will be. Now, she's the kind who'd starve for companionship if she had to live in a place like this. I suppose working, doing her duty, would be different. But to ever consider living here — man, you'd never even dare ask her!"

"Wouldn't I?" Kirk gave up all pretense of courtesy. "Well, Mr. Brad Harrington, that's where you're dead wrong. I intend to. And that's not all. I fully intend that she will — someday — accept."

"You must be crazy!" The well-turned-out doctor looked at the forester in his casual old clothes. "Kelly Lawrence — here? What can you offer her? Mountains, squirrels to talk to?"

"They are high on my asset list. What can you offer her? City streets, pollution, night-clubs, and a fast-paced life?"

"Really, Mr. Long. I don't consider it any of your business. Kelly is *my* fiancée, remember that."

"Kelly will never marry a man she can't respect."

Dr. Harrington turned pale. Looking both ways to see he was not overheard, he demanded, "What did she tell you? Who else knows about it? She promised never to reveal what really happened."

Kirk's heart was singing. His random thrust had drawn blood, far more than he would have dreamed possible. Now to cover up his own lack of knowledge. "I really don't care to discuss the things I have learned, Dr. Harrington." That was true enough.

Shaken, the thinner man hastily retreated. "I think I'll go to my room now, Mr. Long." He turned and walked back to the log house.

"Boy, that was telling him!" Bob and Marilou Campbell grinned at Kirk from behind a clump of trees.

"I didn't know you two were there!"

"Sorry, old man. We were out for a stroll. Didn't know we'd be caught in the position of eavesdroppers."

"It's okay," Kirk said, then noticed Marilou's intent gaze. "What's wrong with you?"

"I'm just wondering if I get to be bridesmaid — and for which groom?" She dodged Bob's grab for her, ran toward their dorm, then called back softly, "May the best man win! Do I hear Kirk faintly say, 'Thanks, I will!'?"

Kirk chuckled in spite of himself.

But Bob only said, "You may have a long hard pull ahead of you, Kirk. That guy looks to me as if he'd be pretty determined, but then with a gal like Kelly — who wouldn't be?" He sighed. "Ah, if only I weren't married to the only truly choice woman in the world, I'd cut both of you out!" And he followed Marilou.

Chapter 10

"Kelly."

From somewhere a voice was calling with the insistence of a summer mosquito, noisily interrupting sleep. Why didn't whoever it was go away, leave her alone? She was so tired; why couldn't she just sleep?

"Kelly." Was the slide starting again? She felt herself being shaken. Her eyes opened in terror, focused, closed again, then opened to look straight into the face of Brad Harrington.

"You?" The four eyes and two moustaches gradually settled into the normal number of features. "Brad? What are you doing here?"

"You asked me to come. Remember?"

With a convulsive effort, she tried to sit up. "I *what?*"

His smile was triumphant. "I knew once you were away from me, you'd see how much you cared. Even so, I was really thrilled when your father told me you needed me badly. I dropped everything and flew."

It began to come back. Her father. "Dad? Where is he?"

"He couldn't come. He told me to give you this." Brad offered her a letter, but Kelly's hands were shaking, too weak to accept it. "Shall I read it?"

"Please." The question still tore through her mind: Why is Brad here? I didn't send for him, I didn't!

Then he began to read.

Dear Kelly,

When you called and asked me to come for a conference on the little boy David I couldn't tell you over the phone why I wouldn't be able to come. There are two reasons:

(1) I am involved on a case here that shouldn't be left, and

(2) I no longer have the total control of my hands I need for the kind of surgery your little friend needs.

I know this will be a shock to you, but arthritis is setting in, and while it doesn't affect a lot of my work, the delicate use of instruments is just too hard. So far none have slipped. But I am always conscious of the fact one might — with disastrous results.

I have asked Dr. Harrington to come, simply telling him you need him. Aside from personal involvements, he is a fine surgeon. He can help David at this point more than I can. He is trained in all my new techniques and will work with your Seattle staff.

Will write more later.

Love,
Dad

Dr. Harrington's eyes were blazing as he dropped the pages. "What a shabby trick! Sending me out here, saying I was needed!"

"You are needed, Brad. David needs your knowledge."

"But your father knew I would think you sent for me, that you —" He choked off the rest of the sentence.

Kelly was too weak to fight. "Maybe he didn't play exactly fair. But would you have come if he had just said there was a patient needing your skill?"

Dr. Harrington had the grace to flush. "Certainly not! I have enough to do in my own hospital. There are just as many kids needing me there as here."

"And now that you're here?"

"I'm flying back out of here as soon as I can go. That oaf at Alpine Meadows said you were going to marry him, and —"

"What!"

"As if you didn't know! He even quoted your exact words when I told him I was your fiancé, that you would never marry a man you couldn't respect! Don't tell me you didn't pass on a certain little incident from the San Antonio hospital! Well, why didn't you tell him the whole story? Or did you?"

"I told him nothing." Kelly was suddenly tired, in spite of her heart whirling like a merry-go-round from his words.

"Then how did he know what happened?"

"I don't know," Kelly said.

Neither of them heard the door open. Neither of them saw the figure that hesitated in the doorway, nailed to the spot by their voices. They were too engrossed in each other.

"You must have told him. Evidently you kept your promise about that the same way you kept your promise about marrying me!"

Red spots of color burned in Kelly's face. "I did keep my promise! Do we have to rehash it all? Even Dad didn't know what really happened in that patient's room."

"All right. Let's talk about what happened. It's between us. We'll clear it up for once and all. Just what did happen?"

Kelly sank back on the pillows, reliving that awful scene. "You ordered medication. I gave it. It was the wrong medication and the patient died from the counter-effects."

"You left out that the patient was terminally ill and the medicine was really a blessing," the doctor said.

The cynicism in his voice angered Kelly beyond belief. Her face caught fire. "I also left out what happened at the investigation." Her voice was low but deadly.

"So I told them it was you who gave the wrong medication," Brad said.

"And you never once added you had ordered it!"

Dr. Harrington's face grew cold. "Any doctor can make a mistake, but when he does it tears down patient confidence in him. After all, what did it matter that I let you take the blame? Once we were married, you wouldn't have been working anyway. And with your father as chief of staff, it could be covered up easily." He refused to meet her eyes squarely.

"Can you imagine the scandal, Kelly, if the truth had come out? Even your father knows I have skill, talent, knowledge. Was all that to be diminished because of one mistake?" He walked to the window. "I had no choice. You know that!"

The phonograph of memory replayed Kelly's words from months before. "No, I suppose for you there was no other choice."

"I can't see why you took it so hard. You were the one who would benefit from my success. I would be able to give you everything you wanted — a home, clothes, prestige. What more could you want out of life than that?"

Her face was sad. "I want a man I can respect."

Dr. Harrington shriveled. Her comment struck home, convincing him beyond doubt she meant what she said. "And I suppose you'll marry this country bumpkin and spend the rest of your life chasing rabbits and squirrels!"

"I don't really see that it concerns you." A wave of color rose through her delicate skin. "But, yes, I may just do that!"

"You *love* this lout?"

Did she? Kelly's eyes closed. Within the space of heartbeats her first meeting with Kirk Long, the subsequent weeks, the growing aversion to Lydia, all rushed through her. Love him? Love Kirk Long?

She remembered opening her eyes on a sandbar, being held close in strong arms, feeling nothing on earth could ever hurt her again. Was this love? It was nothing like the quick flare of emotion Dr. Harrington's suave attentions had won from her.

Was Brad right? Could she in time forget

what he had done, live the life he had laid out for her? What if she went back to San Antonio, left Kirk?

"No! I'll never leave Alpine Meadows — if Kirk wants me!"

The gentle closing of the hospital-room door was lost in her quick protest. She gazed into Brad Harrington's face. "Yes. Yes, I love Kirk Long with every fiber of my being!"

Truth shone from her eyes, rang from the depths of her heart. It caught Brad Harrington unprepared.

He sagged. Then he said, "I pity you." And he turned toward the door.

"Where are you going?"

"Back where I belong, away from this god-forsaken country!"

"What about David?"

"What about him? I owe him nothing."

Kelly's fighting spirit, roused by the recognition of her own love, brought her upright in bed. "No. You owe him nothing. But you do owe me something and I intend it shall be paid."

"Really, Kelly." He stroked the moustache, in control again. "Is this some kind of blackmail?"

"Not at all. Let's just say a favor returned." As his eyes narrowed, she leaned forward. "I let the San Antonio hospital have a field day about the nurse who gave up her job due to a wrong medication. I don't think it's too much to ask that you spend a few days while you're out here, helping an innocent little boy who needs you."

For a long moment he gazed at her. "All right, Kelly. I'll stay."

She sank back in relief. She would be out of the hospital soon. David could be cared for. Then, as far as she was concerned, if she never saw Dr. Harrington again it would be too soon.

Kelly's homecoming was pure joy. The powerful drugs had done their work well. There was only a stout bandage over the cut that was healing beautifully to remind them of the storm and its results.

David had gone back to Seattle for his surgery, promising Kelly he'd be back "sooner." Lydia had gone with him, and so had Tom. The adoption papers had gone through. David Stewart would be getting a new set of parents and a new last name soon.

"We're going to tell him right after the surgery," Tom told Kelly. "We're staying in Seattle until we can bring him back."

Alpine Meadows seemed deserted. Because of Kelly's accident and the Jacksons being gone, Kirk had held off on taking any other campers for a few weeks. Kelly was glad for the rest. She hadn't known how exhausted she really was. She spent a lot of time in the hammock, then went walking, regaining the splendid strength that had been drained that eventful night. Whenever Marilou wasn't with Bob, she dropped by to chat with Kelly.

"Marilou, didn't any of you come see me while I was in the hospital?" Kelly had wondered about it ever since coming home.

"Of course." Her red-haired friend looked surprised. "At first you were out of it. Later, you were occupied with Dr. Harrington. Lydia went in to see you once, but you were busy."

Kelly couldn't quite figure out the odd note in Marilou's words. Besides, it was too much of a blue and gold and green day to worry over it. "I just wondered."

It was during this slack time that Kelly had her fateful little talk with Kirk. She was determined to clear up whatever seemed to have risen between them. Always in her heart she carried the knowledge of what Brad had told her, that Kirk had said he intended to marry her. But if it were true, why had Kirk been so frigidly polite, almost formal since her return?

On the other hand, Brad wasn't imaginative enough to have made up such a tale, especially about a potential rival.

Finally Kelly couldn't stand it any longer. Seeing Kirk crossing the field, she called, "Kirk! Do you have a minute?"

The gladness in his face was instantly masked. "Certainly. Did you need something?"

She couldn't know how earnest her face had grown, how the warm summer day had coaxed flags of color into her cheeks, making them as scarlet as the blouse she wore. Still she stalled.

"When is David coming home?"

She felt like a schoolgirl at the stupid question. Only this morning at breakfast he had reported it would be a few more days.

"Maybe the beginning of next week."

"Oh." Try as hard as she could, she couldn't seem to think of anything else to say.

"Was that all you wanted?" He stood by her hammock, looking down.

Kelly's heart sank. "Well, yes, oh, no!" She plunged in, feeling as if she were in over her head. "Isn't it grand that Dr. Harrington was able to pass on my father's new techniques for David?"

"Yes, it is." His enthusiastic response lowered her spirits immeasurably. He didn't care or he could never endorse Dr. Harrington so heartily.

"You asked him to come, didn't you?" he asked.

"Not exactly. I asked Dad to come and he sent Brad — Dr. Harrington — in his place." She stumbled a bit, unwilling to tell Kirk of her father's growing arthritic condition. "Dad thought I needed Brad. That is, he told Brad that so he'd come, and —"

"I see." Nothing could have been colder than Kirk's brief statement.

Hoping to break through his wall of reserve, Kelly burst out, "You don't see at all, do you? You think Dr. Harrington came on my account."

"Didn't he?"

"Yes, but —"

"Really, my dear, I have a lot to do. Maybe we can pursue this most interesting conversation some other time." Kirk smiled easily and took one step toward the field.

Kelly had heard of brains bursting from sheer fury. Hers would probably be one of them. How could he deliberately be so obtuse? Did she dare throw up to him what Dr. Harrington had told her?

Why not? She'd already acted in such a childish way, Kirk was getting ready to walk

171

off and leave her there. Why not throw caution to the winds?

"Brad said you told him you intended to marry me." The minute the words were out, she regretted them. It sounded like a backhanded proposal!

For a second Kirk's eyes narrowed. Then he laughed, not at all embarrassed. "Oh yes, that. I did."

Kelly couldn't have held back the "Why?" for a fortune.

Kirk laughed again. "You know it's terribly hard to get a nurse up here. Since we've definitely been making plans for a winter sports family camp, it seemed a good way to get one who would stay."

If he had been looking at Kelly instead of gazing out over the lake, he would have seen the color drain from her face.

So all he wanted was a nurse for his precious Alpine Meadows! What of the tenderness, the way he had looked at her sometimes? Kelly hadn't known a heart could ache so much. What should she do? She must never let him know she cared, cared so much she longed to fling herself into his arms.

"I'm afraid that would be quite impossible," she said. Her laugh was a masterpiece of amused tolerance. "I hadn't meant to tell you, but my father plans on coming out in

September. I'll be returning to San Antonio with him when he goes." She wondered at the little smile that played around Kirk's lips. "So you see, though your proposition is so practical, I won't be able to accept."

"You're going back to San Antonio — and Brad Harrington?"

"You might say that." How could he look so indifferent? Kelly's heart sank through her shoes. "I've discovered the mountains are a bit too formidable for me. I'm going back to my sagebrush and rolling hills and prairies. You know, Alpine Meadows is a nice place to visit, but who would want to live here?"

Kirk turned on his heel and walked across the field, slightly bent, making queer choking noises. What on earth was wrong with him? It wasn't until he disappeared around the edge of the big log house that she caught sight of his face. He was laughing — great sobs of laughs being held in!

"I hate him!" All her pent-up emotion flung itself into the words. "I hate him, hate him, hate him! I don't care if I am acting like a child. Why did I have to meet him if I was going to fall in love and have it turn out this way? Dad was right. A man his age who hasn't married doesn't want to. He'd marry me to keep a nurse! Brad was right, too. He's a lout, an oaf, a bumpkin! I can hardly wait to get back to San Antonio and civilization, away from this terrible place!"

But the hate dissolved in the flood of tears she should have cried months before. At last she slept, from sheer exhaustion. She never knew when a tall man with a rugged face quietly slipped back to watch her in the hammock.

"Poor kid. She's had a rough time. I shouldn't have teased her. But she looked so cute." A reminiscent smile lit up his face. He carefully tucked a letter under one relaxed hand and stole away.

Kelly felt better when she awakened. The world hadn't ended. So Kirk didn't love her. She still had her work, didn't she? When her contract was up, she'd find a place where she was needed. Not San Antonio. Maybe Portland. In spite of what she'd told Kirk, she never wanted to leave the Northwest. She loved it.

"From now on I'll need mountains and blue sky and streams," she murmured, then stretched luxuriously. She felt the crackle of paper under her fingers. What was that? It hadn't been there when she lay down.

Another letter from Dad? She pounced on it. It should have his arrival date.

When she finished the letter, she was

stunned. How could she face Kirk Long? Had he known? He must have, the way he laughed. Her face burned as she pictured herself looking up and calmly announcing to Kirk how her father was coming for her, and they were all going back to San Antonio.

Her father was coming, all right, but they weren't going back to San Antonio. The words from Dr. Lawrence's letter were indelibly branded into her brain, flaming red, searing her heart with their import.

. . . and so, Kelly, I have to face the truth. Much as I love my job, the excitement, the thrill of success, I can no longer handle it the way it should be done. I have refrained from letting you know how much this arthritic condition can impair my usefulness until I had made other plans. Now those plans are made.

Kelly, from the time I got your first letter from Alpine Meadows, memories of what the young boy, Kirk, had told me have haunted me. I'm tired, Kelly, terribly tired. These last years have taken their toll. Now I'm ready for a rest.

I know I would never be happy away from medicine except for a short rest.

But I do need that rest. I am going to get it — and keep on with my medicine, too! I have been tremendously interested in Kirk's program there at Alpine Meadows. He assures me the dreams he had are becoming a reality. This year he has proven on a small scale the value of such a camp. Next year he will expand. But the best thing of all — there's a place for me.

And so, Kelly, when I come out, I hope it will be for good. Alpine Hospital has already accepted my offer of help as time permits. I can be there with you on the grounds you have learned to love so much, riding, hiking, swimming — all the things we didn't have enough time for when you were growing up. When the summer season closes, I hope you'll fly home, help me sell our home and move to a new life. . . .

There was more. Offers had already been made for their San Antonio home. Over the protests of the hospital board, Dr. Lawrence's resignation had been accepted.

Kelly put down the letter, too stunned to move. Dad was coming to Alpine Meadows, to be with her, to make a happy life — and she was hopelessly in love with Kirk Long, who cared nothing for her.

The irony of it brought a wave of hysterical laughter up Kelly's throat, to be choked down before it came out in a scream.

A few weeks ago Alpine Meadows had opened its arms to her, the closest thing to heaven she could imagine. Now she could hear the clang of iron bars as the prison it had become clanged behind her, cutting off all hope of escape.

Chapter 11

"I just wanted to say good-bye — oh, excuse me!" Kelly stood horrified in the doorway of the boys' dorm. She had thought Lydia was alone. She hadn't dreamed Kirk Long would be with her and holding the blonde woman in his arms!

If the weeks that had gone by since the arrival of Dr. Lawrence's letter had been hard, this was unendurable. So Kirk was untrue after all, untrue to one of the best friends he had. But how could Lydia act so? She had seemed so content now that David would be hers. She openly walked about with Tom, arms entwined, much as Bob and Marilou walked. Now this.

"It's all right, Kelly." Lydia's eyes were warm. "I was just telling Kirk how happy I am. David's braces are coming off tomorrow! The surgeon tried to contact you, but you were gone. He's going to be able to walk almost without a limp."

Kelly's personal problems were temporarily forgotten. "That's great, Lydia. I hoped it would happen before I went back to San Antonio."

"But you'll be back!" Lydia sounded sincere. "She will be back, won't she?"

Kirk answered both Lydia's appeal and the challenge in Kelly's eyes. "Oh, yes. She'll be back. Dr. Lawrence decided not to come after her, but wait in San Antonio. Something about the sale of the house. We couldn't get along here without our nurse, Lydia. You know that."

There it was again, his need of a nurse. Kelly's lip curled. She had managed to hold in her hurt, hide behind a renewed interest in her work. She had ridden, swum, and hiked with the newest batch of campers. Then September had come, and with it the end of summer and her contract. She was flying to San Antonio Saturday.

I'll never see him again, she thought, turning on her heel and walking out the door. Why should I care? All he wants is a nurse. In spite of what Lydia said, he's probably still half in love with her. The one person he doesn't love is Kelly Lawrence — except for her nursing skill that will help his camp.

Marilou's farewell was typical. "To quote an old phrase, 'Take your time going, but hurry back.' You belong here, Kelly."

Not for worlds would Kelly let her friend see this was the end of Alpine Meadows in her own life. Dad could come on out. She'd get work in a city not far away and meet with him often. But she couldn't stay where she would see Kirk every day. Someday she might be able to accept the pain that had grown to be part of her. Not yet.

"Thanks, Marilou. It's been good knowing you." She snapped the lock on her suitcase. "I have to dash. Kirk's waiting for me."

" 'Bye, Kelly. Come back soon." From the shelter of Lydia's encircling arm David called to her, then broke free and ran to Kelly, giving her a big hug. It almost proved her undoing. She bit her lip hard to steady herself.

" 'Bye, David. You take care of yourself."

Then she was gone, riding down the road to Alpine, to Seattle, away from Alpine Meadows. She wouldn't look back. If she did, she might cry out to the silent man beside her how little she wanted to go. Never again. She had made the opening and he had laughed.

Something of Kelly's thoughts must have been transferred to Kirk. He began to chat of the summer, of all the things that had happened, of how much use she had been. "I can hardly wait until we begin our winter weekends program. If you like it here in summer, wait until you see the leaves falling."

He gestured out the open window. It was a beautiful day with traces of early color showing. "We get reds and golds and oranges you can't believe. I hope you can get back soon before you miss it all. Then winter is white and cold and beautiful. And spring is so unbelievable I won't even try to describe it!"

"You don't really believe I'm coming back, do you?" Kelly couldn't keep the words back.

"Of course. You're coming back and marrying me."

"If you were the last man on earth I wouldn't marry you! I've never known such a conceited, arrogant, selfish man!" She warmed to her subject, never knowing how her flashing dark eyes contrasted with the same red suit she'd worn on her trip to Alpine Meadows.

"Granted. Those are some of the things you'll have to get used to, my dear."

How could you make a dent on a man who wouldn't even argue, who only smiled in an amused way?

"I am not coming back." She spaced each word evenly for emphasis. "I am helping Dad settle things, get him packed. Then I'll start living my own life."

"I know. With me."

Kelly clenched her teeth. "You are maddening, but I didn't think you were totally obtuse. Can't you get it through your thick head I am not going to marry you? All you want is a nurse. Well, go find someone else. I'm not interested."

"Aren't you, Kelly?" Suddenly he was deadly serious. He swung the station wagon off the road, taking a shaded lane, coming to rest under a big tree. Strange how much harder it was to proclaim her independence when he was not driving but looking at her with those blue eyes that could see more than she wanted revealed.

Kelly nervously played with her purse clasp. "I'm going back to Texas where I belong."

"You belong here with me, Kelly." His words were infinitely tender, but she wouldn't look up. The next moment she was in his arms, his lips meeting hers. For one startled second she responded, the love in her heart catching fire from his gentleness. The next she pulled back, opened the car door, and stepped outside.

"Just what do you think you're doing?" There was steel in Kirk's question.

"If you can't leave me alone, I'm walking to where I can get a ride with someone who can."

Angry color shot into his face, giving her

a thrill of satisfaction. Good! She'd teach him to think he could hug Lydia one day and kiss her the next. Red streaks whipped into her cheeks.

Kirk's eyes blazed. With the speed of light he was out of the car. Kelly didn't hesitate. She ran, as if for her life.

"You crazy nut!" In three long strides he caught her, lifted her and dumped her unceremoniously back into the car. "Don't think you can run away from me — not ever!"

She was defeated. She could not make another stand after that. All she could do was hug her corner of the front seat, wishing she could strangle him with her bare hands. If her innate honesty told her that her anger was partly due to her own treacherous response, she ignored the message. She would never forgive him, never.

She would go back to San Antonio and marry Brad Harrington and — she shivered in spite of herself. Not even to show Kirk up would she marry Brad, or anyone else.

"Are we going to Seattle or not?" The coolness of her own voice surprised her.

"Yes. But not until we get a few things understood. When you first came, I told you that when I married a girl, she'd be stuck with me. You're that girl, Kelly. You might as well get used to the idea."

Kelly gasped. "You think you can park out here and give me orders like that? By what right? Who crowned you King of the Royal Mountain?"

"Protest all you like. I know you love me and we'll be married as soon as you and your father return. He's already given his consent. That's why he sent you out here. He hoped I was still single."

Never had Kelly sustained such a shock. Dad? A party to all this? Never!

But Kirk wasn't through. "You ask me by what right I give orders? The right of your fiancé, the man who loves you."

"Fiancé?" She couldn't be hearing him right. "Since when? And you've never once said you loved me!"

"Oh, haven't I? I thought I gave a perfectly good demonstration. Would you like a repeat performance?" His gaiety was even more disturbing than his anger had been.

"Certainly not." Could he hear her heart beating?

"Really, my dear." His sophisticated, amused laugh brought even more color to her already burning face. "I would have thought you would wait until I asked you before announcing the engagement. But since you didn't I would hate to have you embarrassed. So I'll make it formal. Miss Lawrence, will you marry me?"

For one wild moment Kelly thought she would throw her purse at him. To sit there behind the wheel, calmly asking her to marry him as if he were ordering a loaf of bread.

"I repeat, I wouldn't marry you if you were the only man on earth."

"I intend to be — for you." But he started the motor, turned, and swung back toward the main highway.

Some of his comments had only begun to sink into Kelly's brain. "What did you mean — I announced our engagement?"

He looked surprised. "When you were in the hospital. Don't you remember?"

"In the hospital?" Surprise was turning her into a parrot. "Was I delirious?"

"Deliriously happy, I hope."

She subsided. There was no use trying to get answers from this man. She didn't say another word all the way to the airport, although Kirk freely commented on the beauties and advantages of Washington State, especially to a newly married couple. She bit her tongue to keep from answering back. Let him have his fun. He'd see. She'd fly off and he would never find her again.

"Good-bye, Mr. Long." Her ridiculously formal farewell sounded stupid even to her.

"Not good-bye, just so long. I'll be seeing you — sooner than you think."

Now what did he mean by that? There was no time to wonder. Kelly turned on her heel and boarded the jetliner. The smiling stewardess ushered her to a seat and she dropped into it, suddenly worn out. She needed time to think. Yet of all the shocking things Kirk had said, one little phrase repeated itself like a hammer on an anvil, beating into her brain.

Eyes closed, she was only vaguely aware of others crowding the aisles, laughing, happy to be flying home or on vacation, wherever their paths led. Was she the only confused, miserable person aboard?

It wasn't until after the motors were warming, just before time for the stewardess to announce the fastening of seat belts, that she sensed someone dropping down into the seat beside her. She had hoped against hope the seat would remain empty. The last thing she needed was a mouthy seatmate all the way to San Antonio. She purposely kept her eyes closed, even when she felt a rough sleeve brush her arm. But when a strong, masculine hand clasped her own, she sat upright.

"You!"

It couldn't be possible. There sat Kirk Long, a big smile on his face.

"Hello, Miss Lawrence. Fine day, isn't it? Just the day for a busy camp director to take a little time off and fly to San Antonio. I've heard there are quite some sights there. Pretty girls, all that. An old mountain boy like me will have to get used to big city ways."

He made no effort to lower his voice. People in the seats around them were smiling.

Kelly's face felt scorched. If she could only become invisible!

Kirk's voice got louder. "Any chance of having you show me around, Miss Lawrence? Sure would hate to get caught by a city slicker."

"Better help him out, honey," a chubby woman across the aisle advised. "Wouldn't want him to get taken advantage of in the big city of San Antonio!"

"Thank you, ma'am." Kirk doffed his worn sombrero. "Much obliged, I'm sure."

That did it. His impersonation of a country hick released Kelly from the comatose state she had fallen into when discovering him there.

She jerked her hand free. "Sorry, Mr. Long. I'm afraid I'll be otherwise engaged."

What an unfortunate choice of words! It set him off again.

"You know," he confided to the sympathetic woman who had spoken before, "me

187

and my fi-an-cee had a tiff. She wants pink in the nursery, I say blue. Suppose we'd better have twins and use striped wallpaper?"

"Kirk!"

He looked at Kelly as if surprised to see her agony of embarrassment. "Sorry, ma'am. Guess I'd better be mendin' some fences."

But Kelly had turned her face to the window, shutting out the sight of the laughing people around them. How could he? That devil! He was enjoying every minute of making a spectacle of himself, acting like the very country bumpkin Brad Harrington had called him. No one would have believed he was a college graduate, a forestry major, the leader and director of Alpine Meadows.

She whirled back toward him. "You aren't really going to San Antonio, are you?"

"What do you think?" His low voice dropped all pretense. "Isn't it a little late to be getting off?"

They were already airborne, going higher, higher, penetrating the cloud cover that would hide the fall day and Alpine Meadows and Seattle and everything she had come to love, except Kirk himself.

"It's a little late for a lot of things," she said.

"Like telling you I love you?"

Kelly's throat was tight. It took energy to

force out her words. "Especially for that."

"I do, you know." He leaned closer, shutting off the rest of the world as effectively with his words as with his body, blocking the view of other passengers. "I've loved you since you stepped from that plane and told me off."

"Told you off?"

"Sure. Don't you remember? 'I have been working with children ever since I finished training.' I think that was the exact moment I decided to marry you, even though I didn't recognize it until later. Anyone who could stand up to me couldn't be all bad!"

"I don't believe you."

"Don't you?" He gave her a curious look. "Shall I give you another demonstration?" He leaned toward her so purposefully, she automatically held up a hand between them. He caught it, crushed it in his own. "Kelly, you are the woman I want to share my life. The one waiting when I come in at night, the one there when I wake up in the morning. I want a family, kids who will be glad to share Alpine Meadows with others less fortunate. Will you marry me?"

This time there was no amusement or devilment in his eyes. They were open, honest, clear as the lake in the sun with little golden glints in them.

It was true. He loved her. Kelly's heart gave a great leap at his promise for the future.

Mistaking her silence for something other than happiness, Kirk said, "I can't promise all of life will be easy. As I may have told you before, you'll have to learn to live with my stubbornness. After all, an old bachelor like me will have a lot of changes to make."

The plane had risen steadily until it had come out of the cloud cover into brilliant sunshine. Like my life, she thought. Somehow all the uncertainties, misunderstandings, and pain were eclipsed in the tremendous wave of joy that filled her.

"Well? One perfectly good proposal going . . . going . . ."

She could have cried out from the pressure of his fingers on hers.

"Well?" he persisted.

Her answering laugh was shaky. "One perfectly good acceptance going . . . going . . ." Then she boldly asked, "Isn't it customary for newly engaged couples to seal their engagement with a kiss?"

"Here?" He caught the flash of laughter in her eyes, shot a quick look around. "Okay, but I hope no one's looking. I don't believe in necking in public — not even for an engaged couple!" The kiss was quick, but filled with promise.

Kelly's flushed face shone with happiness.

"Say, that's all right! Must have made up your tiff, huh?" the warmly approving woman across the aisle said.

In an instant Kirk was back to his other self.

"Why, shore, ma'am. Me and the missus-to-be can't stay mad long."

Kelly rocked with laughter. Strange how he could change so rapidly! But the laughter broke off abruptly when she felt something cool slide onto her left hand, third finger.

"Kirk!" Her cry was rapturous. "It's beautiful!"

"I thought you might like something a little different. You like red so well, and all." The ring was the loveliest little diamond she had ever seen, surrounded by tiny rubies.

"I love it!"

"Good." He opened a small box. "I thought you might like a plain gold band to go with it — when the proper moment comes!"

Kelly's heart was in her eyes. "I'd love it — when the proper time comes."

When the proper time came they would start a wondrous new life.

Before then, there was much to do, much to arrange. Also, Kelly was to learn that

Lydia had overheard her hospital-room conversation with Brad about the medication mistake in San Antonio. And Lydia had told Kirk.

But deep down Kirk had never really doubted anything about Kelly — as she had never really doubted her love or anything about him.